Bungalow *on* Pelican Way

AN *Emerald Cove* NOVEL

LILLY MIRREN

WELCOME TO EMERALD COVE

Read the series in order...

CHAPTER 1

REBECCA

*T*he slice of carrot cake on the table in front of Rebecca De Vries blurred as she pushed it around with the tines of her fork, and tears filled her eyes. She didn't want to finish eating it, because as soon as she finished eating, it would be time to take Mum and her sister Beth to the airport.

She blinked and glanced up at her mother — short salt and pepper hair, deep brown eyes that crinkled around the edges.

"Penny for your thoughts?" asked Mum.

Rebecca shrugged and set the fork down. "I'm going to miss you, that's all."

Mum reached over the table and took her hand, squeezing it. "I will too. It's been great to spend the past six weeks with you, even though I hate that you were hurt by that beast."

Her sister, Beth, nodded. "The only good thing to

come out of all of this is that Jake is behind bars and won't be able to get out, at least for now, since the judge set the bail so high. I only hope he stays where he is forever."

"So do I, but these things are never certain," replied Rebecca.

Her mother's eyes clouded. "Surely..." she didn't finish her thought, instead releasing Rebecca's hand to dab a napkin at her mouth. "Let's not think about that now. We're celebrating that we get to see you again. I wasn't sure we'd ever have this chance." Her voice choked with emotion. "With you hiding from Jake, we didn't know where you were, if you were okay — at least now we can talk on the phone and spend time together. I wish you'd reconsider moving back home to Manly."

Rebecca chuckled. "I know that's what you want, Mum. And honestly, I'd love to do that. But the fact is, Emerald Cove is my home now. I'm a police officer, I love the people I work with, and of course, there's the beach." She waved a hand to indicate the spectacular view of Emerald Beach they had from their outdoor seating at the Emerald Cafe.

An expanse of golden sand curved around the bay where steady waves curled to the shore, rhythmic and comforting as they shushed into the shallows and bubbled up the sand. A bright sun glanced off the water. Families played in the sand, and children laughed as they jumped and splashed, chasing the waves, then running from them in turn.

"It is a great beach," agreed Beth, her eyes narrowing as she took a sip of her iced coffee. "But we have a beach in Manly too and I'd love you to move back so we could see each other more often."

"I'll visit."

"Do you promise?" asked Beth.

Rebecca nodded. "I promise."

"So, when do you get to testify against the brute?" asked Beth.

"I'm not sure exactly, in a week or so I think. I'm waiting to hear from the barrister. But even though it'll be nerve-wracking, I'm really looking forward to being able to stand up in court again and testify against him. I did it once before, and he managed to worm his way out of the justice he deserved. I don't think he'll be so lucky this time."

"I certainly hope not." Mum's nostrils flared. "He should count himself fortunate that justice isn't handed out by families, because if I could get my hands on him…" She shook her head.

"Thanks Mum, but I'm trusting in the law on this one. I think it'll all work out in the end."

Mum smiled. "Well, I hope you're right. The law didn't help you before, but maybe it will this time."

Rebecca couldn't argue — it was true. The law hadn't protected her all those years when she was on the run from her ex-boyfriend. It wasn't until she agreed to testify against him for the state prosecutor that they offered her protection.

"I suppose we should get moving then or we'll miss our flight." Mum stood to her feet and slung her purse strap over one shoulder.

Rebecca drove them both to the airport, then hugged them and watched as they wheeled their luggage through security. Her mother had stayed with her for the full six weeks of her recovery after she broke her right hand on her ex-boyfriend Jake's jaw when he attacked her.

Beth had joined them a week ago. Rebecca's tiny unit above the fish and chip shop was packed to the brim with suitcases, cosmetics cases, and shoes piled against the walls with three women living there — and she wouldn't have it any other way.

Beth had slept on a blow-up mattress on the lounge room floor and Mum had camped on the pull-out sofa. That morning they'd packed everything away in their luggage and the unit felt empty once again. Rebecca dreaded returning to the quiet unit alone. At least she'd be starting back at work again soon.

The past six weeks was the happiest Rebecca had been in years. She couldn't remember a time when she'd felt so free, so alive. After years of living in hiding from Jake after testifying against him in court, she was grateful to finally be able to live her life without looking over her shoulder or pretending to be someone she wasn't.

She waved a final goodbye as they stopped on the other side of the metal detectors and turned back to look at her. Mum's eyes glistened as she raised a hand to her lips and flung a kiss in Rebecca's direction.

As she walked back to her car, Rebecca shoved her hands deep into the pockets of her shorts and hunched her shoulders against the wind that buffeted her. It smelled of salt, and when hunger pangs pushed the sadness away, she decided not to go home just yet. Instead, she drove to a nearby takeaway place, ordered a hamburger and chips, and sat on the beach to eat.

Several seagulls hopped along the sand nearby, beady eyes studying the proximity of the chips that lay in a small white paper bag at her feet. She waved them away, they took to the air in a flurry of wings, alighting again on their dark-orange claws a few metres away.

The tender beef patty melted in her mouth, and she relished the crunch of lettuce as she bit into the soft bun. Everything tasted better now that her life was her own. The world seemed brighter; she could laugh again without looking over her shoulder to see if Jake was there watching her.

There was one issue that hovered on the edge of her consciousness, disrupting her sleep, and sending her heart into a rapid-fire beat whenever it crossed her thoughts — whether or not the department would let her continue to work as a police officer in Emerald Cove.

She'd been stationed there as part of her cover. It'd been her only request when she'd agreed to testify against her criminal ex-boyfriend — that she could work as a cop. It was something she'd always wanted to do, and, she'd reasoned, he'd never look for her in a police station.

It was a nice idea at the time, but he'd found her anyway. She still didn't know how — perhaps a leak in the department, maybe luck. Whatever it was that led him to her, the moment he broke into her unit and confronted her everything had changed.

She'd been put on administrative leave pending the completion of the investigation, and also to give her hand a chance to heal. When she asked how long it would take, she'd been given a vague answer — maybe six weeks or so.

Rebecca swallowed the last bite of burger and scrunched the paper bag with one hand as she pushed to her feet. She wiped the sand from her rear with her free hand and hiked back up the beach to her car.

Her only consolation in the entire process was that her boss, Franklin, had assured her he'd stand up for her. That he'd make sure they knew how much of an asset she'd been to the team in her short time in Emerald Cove.

Even hearing him say that had filled her heart with warmth. Franklin's taciturn manner meant she was never sure what he thought of her, and there'd been a time when he hadn't been so happy to have her on his team.

She threw the rubbish in a nearby bin, then started the car with a sigh. She'd find out what the future held for her soon enough. It'd been so long since she'd felt as though she belonged somewhere. She'd met Jake in Sydney when she was seventeen years old, ten long years ago; her life since that moment had been a horrifying sequence of dramatic upheavals, angry outbursts, beatings and abuse, trips to the hospital, starting over somewhere new, and Jake finding her to begin the cycle again.

It was hard for her to believe that it was finally over. He no longer had a hold on her, couldn't find her, reach her, or hurt her anymore. She'd lived on the run, alone and afraid for so long, she wasn't entirely sure how to live any other way. But she was looking forward to learning.

CHAPTER 2

FRANKLIN

*T*he computer screen flashed as a blank report loaded, and the cursor blinked at Franklin Russell, waiting for him to type. With a grunt, he ran a hand over his dark curls. He couldn't focus. He hadn't been able to think straight about much of anything for days.

He leaned back in his chair and linked his fingers behind his head. His thoughts kept returning to the same subject over and over, even when he was out on a call or trying to sleep in in his too quiet house at night — Proby.

Bec had been away from the office for weeks and as much as it pained him to admit it, things weren't the same around there without her. He'd been angry when the brass in Sydney assigned her to the Emerald Cove station as his partner — told them he didn't need a partner, didn't want one either. But the truth was, he hadn't wanted her to replace his best friend and former partner who'd died on the job. And nothing about that was her fault.

There was a tap on his office door. He straightened in his seat. "Come in."

Steph, the station's receptionist, peeped around the door with a smile, her red curls piled high on her head in a messy ponytail. "Hey, boss. How's things?"

He waved her to a seat across from him. "Things are… things are good. Quiet."

Her lips pursed. "Because Bec is gone?"

He shook his head, reached for the mouse to click absently at the report on the screen. "Of course not, I mean because there hasn't been much going on lately."

"Right," she agreed. "Anyway, I brought that paperwork you wanted me to copy for you. Here it is." She thrust a stack of papers onto his desk but didn't otherwise move.

"Anything else?" he asked, quirking an eyebrow.

"I was wondering when we'll find out about Bec — if she can come back here to work?" Her green eyes wide, she watched him for a response.

"I'm not sure exactly. She has to go to Sydney to testify and the brass want to talk to her while she's down there. They've been pretty close-lipped about the whole thing, I'm not in the loop but I'll make sure the team knows as soon as I'm able to share anything."

She nodded. "Thanks."

He waited.

"You miss her, don't you?" pressed Steph with a grin.

His eyes narrowed. "For heaven's sakes! Doesn't anyone have any work to do around here?"

She jumped to her feet. "Of course, thanks, boss."

When she was gone, he gave up the pretence of completing the report on his computer and leaned back in his chair again, rubbing his eyes with his fingertips. What he needed was some action, something going on around town to keep him distracted. The idea that the head office might not let Bec stay in Emerald Cove was eating at his nerves. He'd spent months training her; if he had to replace her with some new Proby now after all the effort he'd gone to... well, he wouldn't be happy about it and he'd make sure they heard from him.

That was the only reason this whole thing was bothering him — he didn't want to have to break in a new Proby. It'd been hard enough to get Bec to the point where she was a useful officer, a valuable member of their small team.

The fact that everyone around him seemed to infer more than that about their strictly professional relationship wasn't of concern to him. He had other things to worry about than what a bunch of gossips had to say.

Constable Phil Conway stuck his head through the door. "We've got a pile-up on the Pacific Highway, Sarge."

Franklin leapt to his feet, reached for his hat, and shoved it on his head. "Let's go."

THE ACCIDENT SCENE stretched for about one hundred metres along the edge of the highway. Traffic had begun to thicken as rubberneckers crept past the wreckage.

By the time Franklin arrived in his police cruiser,

local firemen were already on the scene, two bright red fire trucks with lights flashing parked nearby on the verge.

"Set up a perimeter and get this traffic sorted," barked Franklin as he stepped out the car.

"Yes, Sarge," replied Phil, hurrying away.

"And call Tweed Heads for more back up, we're gonna need it," he shouted after the departing Constable's back.

Phil waved a hand over his head to indicate he'd heard Franklin's command.

From Franklin's initial count it looked as though at least five cars were involved in the accident. Some in worse shape than others. One vehicle lay on its roof, which was where the firies were concentrated. Franklin strode to the car, his mind in overdrive as he took in the scene.

"What have we got?" he asked, squatting beside the overturned vehicle to look past the fireman's shoulder and into the cab.

"Two trapped inside, both non-responsive. We're getting the jaws of life ready to pull them out. Haven't had a chance to check on the others lately, but when we arrived, they were all conscious from what I could see."

"I'm on it," replied Franklin.

As he ran to the next vehicle, he jumped over a twisted bumper, his heel crunching on the remains of a headlight. Smoke issued from the rear of the blue sedan closest to him. He aimed in that direction, reached it, and leaned through the open passenger window. Inside he found two men, one with his eyes closed and the other clutching at his chest with a grimace.

"You two okay?" he asked.

The man in the driver's seat glanced at him, his face twisted in pain. "My chest hurts." He groaned, leaned back, the seat belt taut against his torso. A deflated airbag hung in his lap like a week-old balloon.

"What's your name?"

"I'm Harold."

"Pleased to meet you, Harold. Can you unclip your seat belt?"

The man reached for it, and the seat belt fell slack.

"And what about your friend?" asked Franklin.

The man looked at his companion in the passenger seat as if seeing him for the first time. Grey hair fell in a clump across his eyes and he pushed it back.

"Ron? You awake?" He reached out a hand and pushed the man's shoulder gently. "He was awake a few minutes ago. Talked to me about something. I can't recall what it was."

While they were talking Franklin checked Ron's vital signs. His pulse was weak, his breathing shallow. There was a deep slash across the man's forehead that oozed red blood. "That's okay. Let's see if we can get you out of there, and I'll find a paramedic to help Ron."

Franklin helped him out of the car and found him a safe place to sit. Then, he got on his radio to call for a paramedic. He was informed the first ambulance would be on the scene in a few minutes, as it'd been held up by the traffic backing up along the highway.

He asked Phil to make sure the ambulance came straight ahead to the blue sedan, then crouched back down on his haunches to study the vehicle. It'd obviously rolled, as the roof of the car was crushed and the sides were battered.

With a grunt, Franklin leaned into the car through

the open window. He pulled on the lever to open the door, but it wouldn't budge. He peered down to see Ron's leg seemed to be pincered between two pieces of the splintered dashboard.

Behind him, an ambulance pulled into the empty space between two vehicles, lights flashing. Steven and his partner climbed out and hurried to where Franklin squatted. He stood to meet them.

"Afternoon Sarge. Update?" asked Steven.

Franklin filled them in on Ron's situation. Steven checked his vitals, just as Franklin had done minutes earlier.

"We've got to get him out of there. Looks like it's up to us, since the firies are busy."

"Yep, we'll have to figure this one out. I'm going to climb in the driver's side."

Franklin rounded the end of the car and noticed fluid dripping from the undercarriage. He leaned down to peer beneath the car. The stench of petrol filled his nostrils. His lips pursed. They had to get Ron out of the car, and fast.

"We've got spilled fuel over here, and there was smoke issuing from the exhaust a little while ago. We should hurry," he said as he slipped into the driver's seat.

"I'm going to tell the firies what's going on," said Stephen, and he ran off in the direction of the nearest fire truck.

Franklin began to talk to Ron, even though he was still unconscious. He used a soothing tone as he unclipped the man's seatbelt and positioned himself with arms around Ron's chest.

He was acutely aware that if Ron had neck or spinal damage, he could be making things worse by tugging him from the vehicle. But if the fuel caught fire, they'd both die in the flames. He had to get Ron out of there fast, there was no other choice.

With as gentle a movement as he could manage, he shifted Ron's position so that the man was leaning towards the driver's side door. Then, he pulled slowly, shifting the man over the centre console.

When the fuel caught fire at the back of the car, he heard it rather than saw it. His heart thundered on a spike of adrenaline.

"Sorry, Ron mate, we've got to move a bit faster. I hope it doesn't hurt too bad." He hauled Ron over the driver's side seat even as the heat of flames licked the back seat of the car.

The fire spread quickly, faster than he could've imagined. By the time he got Ron out the door, the flames roared with delight over the headrests, fanned by the hot wind that had picked up pace as it blew in from the coast and along the highway.

He threw Ron onto his back and struggled up the steep embankment beside the highway. People shouted, ran in every direction. He couldn't hear what they were saying, all he heard was the sound of his own heart beating loudly in his ears, and the rush of breath filling his lungs as he puffed his way up the bank.

When Ron lay safe at the top of the bank, Franklin turned to face the accident scene below, expecting to hear the thunder of an explosion at any moment, to feel the heat and rush of wind as it knocked him from his feet. Instead, he saw a pair of fire fighters in fire retardant suits extinguishing the flames.

He fell to the ground, still puffing hard. Steven

rushed over to him pale-faced. "There you are. I thought you were still in the car. You're okay?"

Franklin nodded. "I'm fine. Ron could do with some help though."

He and Steven wheeled Ron on a trolley to the back of the ambulance and loaded him in.

"Is he gonna make it?" asked Franklin.

Steven slammed the back doors shut. "Not sure, he could have internal damage. But we'll get him to the hospital as fast as we can. If he lives, it'll be because of you."

Franklin offered him a weary smile. "Just doing my job."

Steven grinned. "You and Bec both, huh? The two of you are like superheroes."

He watched, hands pressed to his hips, as the ambulance pulled away in the direction of the hospital, siren blaring. Another soon followed in its wake. He surveyed the accident scene — there was more work to be done. He jogged to the next car, clearing his mind to prepare for whatever he might find there. This was what he loved, it was what he lived for — helping people in their darkest times, doing everything he could to make sure they made it through the worst day of their lives. And there was nowhere else he'd rather be.

CHAPTER 3

CINDY

*T*he small white Pomeranian stood by the back door, peering at her through the glass. Cindy Flannigan glanced over her shoulder once, sighed, and hesitated in her descent down the stairs.

"I'll be back before you know it, Petal," she called.

The dog cocked its head to one side.

Cindy smiled to herself as she continued towards the garage and climbed into her silver Camry. At least someone cared whether or not she was at home. It was hard for her to come to terms with the fact that at sixty-one years of age she lived alone with Petal, a fluffy, white Pomeranian she'd owned for eight years. The two of them rattled around in a house that was far too big for them but was where she'd raised her family with the husband who'd deserted her for his much younger assistant a year earlier.

The engine purred to life and she pulled out of the

garage, raising one hand above her head to hit the remote that released the door behind her. She crept down the long, curving drive and onto the road, careful not to scrape the underside of the car on the high curb. The car swept past the regal *Seaside Manor Bed and Breakfast* where Emily and Cindy's son Ethan were hosting their first large wedding in the new pagoda he'd built in the garden, and towards the small, seaside town of Emerald Cove.

When she pulled into the parking lot behind the Emerald Cafe, her phone rang in her purse. She pushed her greying blond bob behind one ear as she answered it, setting the car in park.

"Adele, my darling, how are you?"

"I'm okay. Where are you?"

Cindy tucked her purse beneath her arm, her phone against her ear and climbed out of the Camry. "Heading into the cafe. What about you? Do you have any flights today?"

"No, it's my day off." Adele sighed.

"Everything okay?" Cindy stood still. Something was wrong; she could always tell when one of her children was upset. And her mum radar was shrilling.

"I don't know. I'm fine I guess. I'm not sick or anything. But I've been a bit low lately."

"What does that mean? What's wrong?" asked Cindy, her entire body tensing. One of the hardest parts about having her youngest child live as far away as Darwin meant that most of the time she had no idea what was going on in Adele's life. She was so out of the loop it sometimes brought a rush of panic that made her breath catch in her throat to think of her baby all alone, flying planes all over the country from that far-off city.

"I haven't felt like myself for a while. I didn't want to say anything to you about it, didn't want to worry you, but my therapist said I should be more open about my struggles."

"Therapist?" Cindy's eyes widened. "I didn't know you were seeing a therapist, love. Now I'm getting worried."

"Yeah, I've been going to weekly sessions for about six months."

"I wish you'd told me." Cindy slumped against the side of the car.

"I couldn't. I was down in the dumps, feeling sorry for myself, I couldn't bear you thinking I was a failure on top of all that."

"Oh love, I'd never think that about you. You should know that. I want you to be able to tell me anything. I'm so sorry I wasn't there for you, but I'm here now."

"Thanks, Mum. I hate to upset you. You've got enough going on in your own life with Dad leaving. Now he's moved back to town with Keisha, and I know that's a big deal for you."

Cindy's heart tightened. "I don't want you to hold things inside because you're worrying about me. I'm the mother, it's my job to worry about you. And besides, I'm fine about Dad and Keisha moving home to the Cove. I'm happy for them." She grit her teeth as she spoke, willing her words to be true.

"Well, if you're sure."

Adele's voice was soft, a lethargic monotone. It wasn't like her. Usually Cindy's youngest child was vibrant, bubbly, and full of life.

"I'm certain."

"It's so lonely up here. Don't get me wrong, there're

plenty of people around, but I can't seem to work up the enthusiasm to be a part of anything that's going on. I want to, but I don't have the energy. It all sounds dull, disappointing. Oh, I don't know — I'm sure I sound crazy."

Cindy swallowed around a lump forming in her throat. "No, not crazy at all. I know how that feels. But I'm concerned about you being up in Darwin all alone. You should come home, spend some time with the family."

"My work is here," objected Adele.

"There's plenty of work on the Gold Coast, and besides work isn't everything. You can help out at the cafe, if you want — that will give you something to do. And I can take care of you, or at least keep an eye on you." She couldn't bear the thought of her baby living alone and depressed in a strange city, so far away.

"I'll think about it," replied Adele.

Cindy exhaled and combed fingers through her hair. "Good. I'm glad. I'll give you a call later. Okay?"

She hung up the phone and squeezed her eyes shut for several moments, her heart aching at the pain she'd heard in Adele's voice.

When her eyes blinked open, she took in the sights and sounds of the street. Emerald Cove was her home. It had been for all of her life. She'd inherited the *Emerald Cafe* from her parents when they died, and it'd become her refuge from a troubled marriage. Still, she was sixty-one and not in as good shape as she'd been even five years ago. She should spend more time in the gym or walking on the beach, but lately she'd been so busy with everything going on in her life she hadn't been looking after herself as much as she should.

The cafe was busier than ever, and it seemed to

take up most of her time to manage it these days. Besides that, there was always a staff member out sick, or on leave, or unable to get to work on time and invariably she'd find herself filling in for them as well as doing all of her own tasks.

It was taking a toll on her. Perhaps if Adele came home and helped out at the cafe it'd remove some of the strain from Cindy, as well as being a way for her to make sure her daughter was okay. If she came home, Adele wouldn't be lonely — she'd have the entire family close by, as well as all her old friends.

The more she thought about it, the more certain Cindy became that it was the best thing for Adele. Her daughter could move back in with her, and work at the cafe.

With a resolute bob of her head, she straightened her shoulders and set off towards the cafe. Her gaze landed on a woman pushing a shopping trolley away from Foodstore on the opposite side of the road.

Panic flickered in her chest.

Keisha.

Her ex-husband's new girlfriend. *New* probably wasn't the most accurate word to describe a woman he'd likely had a long affair with while Cindy was still married to him. But if she burrowed too far into that line of thinking it only made her angry, and there was no sense in getting all worked up over something she couldn't control. It was old news anyway.

She ducked her head and increased her pace. If she could get behind the vine covered fence of the cafe's outdoor seating area Keisha might not see her and she could avoid an awkward encounter.

She'd told herself she wasn't upset about Andy and Keisha returning to Emerald Cove, but the fact was

19

she'd been dreading their first run-in ever since Andy told her about the move. It was a small town, tiny in fact, until the swell of summer visitors doubled its size. There was no way she'd be able to avoid them forever, but she could certainly do her best.

Just as she reached the corner of the cafe, she heard her name being called.

"Cindy!"

It was Andy. She'd recognise his voice anywhere. With a sigh, she wrinkled her nose, then plastered a smile to her face and spun towards him.

"Andy, Keisha, how lovely to see you."

Andy had lost the extra kilograms he'd been carrying around his waist for the past twenty years. He wore a smart aqua polo tucked into a pair of dark denim jeans. Keisha was as loudly fashionable as always in a knee-length, floral print cotton dress with spaghetti straps. The colours accentuated her naturally golden tan, and long, black hair. Her brown eyes narrowed as they fixed on Cindy, and she tossed her head, flashing a brilliant white smile.

"Cindy, you haven't changed a bit."

She wasn't sure if that was an insult or a compliment, but she chose to take it as the latter. The last thing she wanted was to make things even more awkward between them. But Keisha had always been one to offer backhanded compliments, even when she'd worked as Andy's assistant at his financial planning business before their affair.

"Well, thank you Keisha. You look wonderful too."

Cindy clutched her purse, unsure of whether to hug her ex in greeting, or shake Keisha's hand like a teenager on a job interview. Her heart skittered in her chest.

"I was wondering when we'd run into you," said Andy.

"Well, you know me, busy, busy, busy." Cindy issued a burst of laughter that felt as strange as it sounded. She cleared her throat. "How did the move go?"

Keisha rolled her eyes. "Disaster. We went through three moving companies before we found someone who was suitable. No one can do a good job these days, so much incompetence. It's astounding, really. But we have so much stuff, too much — I always tell you that, don't I Andy?"

He nodded obediently.

"Anyway, some of it is very valuable. I don't like cheap things, I want to buy furniture, decorations and stuff that are worth something. You know what I mean?" She sighed. "Oh sorry, you probably don't understand. I know you like the simple life, but not me."

Keisha looped one arm through Andy's and stroked his bicep with pink tipped fingers. "No, the simple life isn't for me. I like the finer things. Right honey?"

Another nod from Andy, whose cheeks reddened.

Cindy's lips pursed. "That's nice."

Andy's obvious discomfort at least gave Cindy some satisfaction. Perhaps he was finally recognising Keisha's rudeness for what it was. In the past when she'd tried to bring it to his attention, he'd denied it was a problem, and insisted instead that it was simply Cindy's sensitivity that was to blame.

"Well, I suppose I should get going. I've got a million things to do at the cafe," said Cindy, tapping her watch with a finger.

Andy smiled. "Of course, I'm sure we'll see you around town."

"Seems inevitable," replied Cindy with a wave.

As she walked back across the street to the cafe, her stomach clenched with irritation. She couldn't let Keisha get under her skin. It was exactly what she'd always done with Cindy, treated her as though she were somehow lesser. That staying home to raise children, pottering in her garden, even baking — all the things Cindy loved to do, were pointed out and ridiculed in Keisha's passive aggressive way.

As she slumped into the chair behind her desk in the tiny cafe office, she steepled her fingers and shook her head. If only Andy hadn't moved back to the Cove, she could've continued to ignore the fact that he'd moved on with a younger woman. But now that they were living close by, she'd have to face up to the fact that her husband hadn't cared enough about her to spend their golden years together. And as much as she was completely aware of all of his failings, that was the thing that pained her the most. They'd shared so much of their lives together, but he'd abandoned her to spend her older years alone. At least she had her children and her friends. But still, Andy's betrayal was hard for her to get past.

CHAPTER 4

REBECCA

*T*he cozy white kitchen smelled of disinfectant. Tiles gleamed beneath her feet. She studied them, legs crossed at the ankles while she waited. The kettle boiled, the water churning with the effort before switching itself off and falling silent. Rebecca reached for it and poured boiling water into two cups over the waiting tea bags.

"Milk?" she asked.

Franklin shook his head and took a cup into his hands, leaned against the bench. She'd come to the office to talk to Franklin about her return to work. The station was quiet. Only she and Franklin were there, besides Steph who sat at the reception desk. They stood in the office kitchen with an awkward space between them. She wasn't used to this type of relationship, one where they discussed things and smiled politely. Usually, Franklin called her *Proby* and shouted at her to do this or that, she told him *yes, boss* and jumped to it. Rebecca was too nervous to sit. She fidgeted with the handle on the nearest drawer, then pulled it out and found a spoon to stir milk into her tea.

"So, are you ready to come back to work?"

She cocked her head. "I can't wait. But head office says I have to take time off until they've done an investigation. It's so frustrating. I'm sitting around at home by myself. I take walks on the beach, I go to boxing but can't box because of my hand — so instead I skip rope, do sit ups and stuff, and then go home again. I eat alone, I sleep alone." She grunted with frustration. "Then it all starts over again. I miss being here, having something to occupy my time."

"I'd get you into the office to do paperwork, but honestly there's not much to do."

"They wouldn't let me do it, anyway. They haven't decided yet if I can keep working as a cop after everything that happened with Jake." She took a sip of tea, her stomach churning with the thought that maybe she'd have to leave this place permanently if head office decided she was too much of a liability.

"So, you're off to Sydney to testify?" asked Franklin.

His brown eyes met hers, and she fought the urge to embrace him. She missed working alongside him every day as partners, missed his sarcasm, his humour, and even his grumpy comments.

"Yep. Sydney today, then I'll stay with Mum for a little while. I'll be back in a few days. Hopefully, after that, I'll be allowed to return to work."

"We'll be here."

* * *

24

REBECCA WAITED by the baggage claim conveyer, her one small rolling bag by her feet. Crowds scuttled by. The atmosphere was different in Sydney than it was at the Gold Coast airport. More hurried, frantic. People wore suits and pulled roller bags after them, striding with purpose over the shiny tiled floor. It was clear people had things to do and places to be, unlike the travelers wearing t-shirts and board shorts she'd left behind. Soon she saw her mother weaving through the crowd. She waved to Rebecca, puffing as she hurried over to hug her.

"Sorry I'm late. I got caught in traffic."

"No worries," replied Rebecca, kissing Mum's cheek. "I haven't been here long."

"It's good to see you back home again."

"It feels good to be home. I wasn't expecting all of these emotions, but flying over Sydney, stepping out of the plane — I couldn't help shedding a few quiet tears. I can't wait to get this trial over so I can go back to my normal life. But I am glad to be here — at least I can spend some more time with you and Beth. I had so much fun showing you both around Emerald Cove."

Mum grabbed the handle of Rebecca's luggage and began to pull it to the exit doors. "It was wonderful. You've built a lovely life for yourself up north. And I won't say another thing about you moving home."

Rebecca chuckled. "Thanks, Mum."

Mum's short, brown hair was flecked with grey. Her green eyes had more lines around them than before Rebecca had gone on the run from Jake. It was hard knowing she'd lost so much time with her family while she was hiding from her ex. He'd stolen so much from her over the years. She was grateful she'd get the chance to testify against him and hoped it would mean she'd never have to worry about him coming after her again.

On the drive home to Manly, Rebecca and her mother barely paused to take a breath. Mum updated her on everything going on in their neighbourhood. Who'd gotten a divorce, the women who'd had babies or were pregnant, the new basketball court built at the local school. Rebecca smiled as she listened, glad to have life back to normal, at least for a moment. It was as though she'd emerged from a deep, dark tunnel into the light.

* * *

THE COURTROOM WAS empty except for a few people Rebecca didn't recognise: the solicitors, their assistants, and a young man she assumed was the court clerk, organising some paperwork on an imposing oak desk.

Rebecca walked through the double doors in the back of the room, her footsteps muted by the navy carpet that covered the courtroom floor. She scanned the room nervously until her gaze landed on the back of the soliciting advocate's head. Julia Simmons was prosecuting the case against Jake, and she'd prepped Rebecca for the types of questions she expected the defence to ask. Still, Rebecca wrung her hands together until her knuckles whitened as she made her way to the seat behind Julia.

Julia spun about on her seat when she heard Rebecca's greeting. She smiled, stacking sheets of paper with both hands.

"Rebecca, there you are. Are you ready?"

Rebecca swallowed. "I think so."

"No one's with you?"

She shook her head. "Mum wanted to come, but I asked her not to. I don't need anyone else here to make me even more nervous than I am already. I just want this to all be over so I can get started on my life."

Rebecca crossed one leg over the other as Julia continued to go over her notes with her assistant. She watched as the jury filed in to fill the seats along one side of the courtroom. Finally, the judge entered, a woman wearing a grey wig and flowing black robes. She sat at the oak desk without looking up, whispered a few things to the court clerk, then began the proceedings with a thump of the gavel.

Much of what happened next was something of a mystery to Rebecca. There was a lot of legal talk, solicitors standing up, sitting again, and things going back and forth. There were instructions to the jurors, and a few motions. She'd spent some time in the magistrates' office in Emerald Cove but hadn't been in a court room often. She knew how the process worked in theory, but seeing it in action, it was hard to keep up.

Finally, it was time for Julia to call the prosecution's witnesses and Rebecca was the first. She knew from speaking with Franklin that he'd be testifying the next day. He would fly to Sydney in the morning, then back to the Cove in the afternoon since he couldn't afford to take more time off work with her still on leave.

She walked to the witness stand, wiping her wet palms down her slacks. By the time she was asked the first question, the only thing she could think about was that Jake was watching her. He sat behind plexiglass in the defendant's chair, his blue eyes fixed on her, lips drawn into a smirk. One dimple danced in his chiseled cheek. Once upon a time that dimple, the half-smile, would've fooled her. She'd have thought him charming, sexy — not now. Now she saw the cold anger behind his ice blue eyes, the tension in his jaw.

She swallowed as Julia walked towards her, shuffling papers. The solicitor looked up, smiled, and stopped directly in front of her.

"Thank you for being here, Constable De Vries. I know this must be very difficult for you, after everything you've been through."

"Objection!" called the defending solicitor.

Julia didn't so much as flinch. She simply glided into the next question.

"Never mind, I have a question for you, Constable. When did you first meet the defendant?"

Julia walked her through their prepared questions one by one, and by the time they'd gotten to the subject of the attack, the muscles across Rebecca's shoulders had softened and the sweat coating her body had cooled.

She could do this.

"How did you feel when you received the threatening email from the defendant?" asked Julia as she strode to the table and reached for a glass of water to take a sip.

"Objection, Your Honour, it hasn't been established that any communication from my client was threatening in nature."

"Sustained. Ms. Simmonds, please keep the emotional rhetoric to a minimum." The judge peered over half-moon glasses perched on the end of her long nose.

Julia offered a swift nod. "Yes, Your Honour."

"I was horrified. I'd built up this whole life in

Emerald Cove, a life I believed he knew nothing about. I'd been working as a police officer, had made friends, had found a place to live across from the beach. For the first time in years, I felt safe. But when the email came, I knew he'd found me, and it was just a matter of time before I saw him."

"And what did you think he might do?"

"Objection, what the witness thinks my client might or might not do is hardly relevant," the man at the defendant's table almost shouted.

"It speaks to the history my witness has with the defendant."

"Overruled, continue."

Julia's smile widened. "You can answer, Constable."

"I knew what he'd do, because he'd done it so many times before. He'd come to see me, and at first he'd be charming, friendly, act like nothing had ever gone wrong between us, then, after a little while, when I didn't do what he wanted me to do, he'd get violent."

"Violent?"

"Yes, he beat me many times. I ended up in the hospital on three separate occasions over the years we were together and then again after I left him, when he found me."

"The hospital. That sounds like he was quite vicious?"

"Yes, he was." Rebecca was surprised by how calm she felt. She'd been worried that talking about what'd happened between them would make her too emotional to be able to continue, or that she'd feel so ashamed she wouldn't want to. Instead, she felt strong, resilient, at peace. It was finally time to tell the court what Jake had done to her, how he'd ruined her life. It was time for him to go to jail to pay for his crimes.

She glanced at the jury as she spoke and found sympathy in their eyes. They watched her with what seemed to be an intense interest in what she had to say. Julia gave her a little nod to encourage her to keep going. And so, she did. She told them everything, let it all spill out, and as she did, a huge weight lifted from her shoulders, floated over her head, and disappeared out the double doors at the front of the courtroom.

CHAPTER 5

FRANKLIN

*T*he knife in Franklin's hand slipped and he sliced the tip of his finger. Blood spurted out, and he swore, grabbed a paper towel, and pressed it to the wound. He leaned against the kitchen bench in his quiet single-story brick home and shook his head.

He hadn't been focused on the job at hand. He was dicing sirloin steak to go in the beef and vegetable stew he was making for dinner for himself and his father, but his mind was elsewhere. He couldn't help worrying about Rebecca and the court case. He was headed to Sydney in the morning to testify and had hoped she'd call him after she'd finished win court. But, so far, he hadn't heard from her, even though he'd checked his phone for a missed call or message at least fifty times that evening.

The good thing was that after everything that'd

happened to her, and after their encounter with Jake in her unit, the scumbag was finally going to be put behind bars. But a single thought jangled in the back of his mind that he couldn't ignore — he'd been involved in these kinds of cases many times over his years on the force, and there was no certainty. Especially when a jury was involved. There was no way of knowing how the verdict might go, or what sentence the judge would hand down even if Jake was found guilty. And if Jake was released right away, or even in a few years' time, what would happen to Rebecca then?

The thing he hated most about all of it was that there was nothing he could do. He couldn't control the outcome of the trial, couldn't protect Rebecca from her ex. The only thing he could do was to give his testimony to the best of his ability; after that, it was completely out of his hands. And he hated it.

He finished chopping vegetables and used the sharp edge of his knife to push them from the cutting board into the pot, then seasoned the stew, tasting the final result with a wooden spoon. With a grunt of approval, he headed for his bedroom. His neatly made bed, with its brown corduroy doona greeted him and he eyed it with a shake of his head. He'd always believed he'd get married one day and share this house he'd worked so hard to buy with a family. But the years had passed by, relationships had come and gone, and still he lived alone now that his father had been moved into a nursing home after a stroke left him unable to care for himself while Franklin was at work.

As he peeled off his uniform and stepped under the hot jets of water from the oversized shower head, he wondered how his life had gotten so far off the track he'd envisioned. By now he'd imagined himself a father, taking his son to *Nippers*, the junior surf life-saving club, or his daughter to gymnastics classes, on his days off.

Instead, somehow, he'd ended up completely alone. Even his best friend was gone. He cared about the team he worked with, and they him, but being the boss was a lonely profession, even in such a close-knit police community. He found himself missing Rebecca — she'd been off work now for almost two months, and he hadn't realised how much her presence had cheered him and given purpose to his days. She wasn't much for talking, but having her riding with him in the cruiser helped the time to pass more quickly and gave him something to look forward to each day.

The hot water coursed over his head and down his back, working out some of the tension that'd lodged in his muscles throughout the day. Finally, he switched off the water, dried himself and dressed in a pair of jeans and a T-shirt.

By the time he'd driven a Tupperware container full of stew from his bungalow over to the nursing home, he was almost too late for visiting hours but hoped they wouldn't mind. He missed having his father living at home with him, and the guilt of not being able to care for him lodged like a stone of pain in Franklin's throat as he walked through the quiet halls to his father's room.

Since the stroke, his father had made so much progress. He was able to talk, although the muscles on one side of his face still sagged. He could walk with help from the nursing staff, and he was back to eating the same kinds of foods he'd always loved. Franklin had been amazed by how quickly the nursing and physiotherapy teams had managed to help his father take all of these steps in only a couple of months.

"Hey, Dad," he said in a soft voice as he stepped through the doorway.

His father was watching television from an armchair in one corner of the room.

"Franklin, I was wondering if you'd be coming over. I asked the nurses not to bring tea, but my stomach is rumbling, and I was getting worried." His words slurred, but the meaning was clear enough to Franklin's ear.

His lips pulled into a half smile rather than the wide grin he usually offered Franklin, but the sight of him still warmed Franklin's heart. He set the food down on a small round table and leaned in to give his dad a hug.

"You know I wouldn't forget you."

"I know that, but sometimes your work needs your whole attention."

"That's true," admitted Franklin. "But I'd make sure someone fed you. I made stew."

"I love your stew."

"I know you do. I've missed having you at the house, Dad. I wish…"

His father's brow furrowed. "I don't think I can come back, son. I'm sorry — it'd be too hard on you. It's too much to expect you to take care of an old codger like me."

Franklin's throat closed over. He coughed. "No, it's not too much. I'd rather you were at home."

"I think that decision is out of our hands now, mate," replied Dad, squeezing Franklin's hand with his own blue-veined, arthritis-ridden one.

Franklin shook his head. "I'm sorry, Dad. I wish I had a nine to five job."

Dad sighed. "It wouldn't matter, and I don't want that for you. You love your job."

"I love *you*," replied Franklin, clearing his aching throat again.

Dad's eyes glistened. "I couldn't love you more, or be more proud of you."

Franklin set about spooning the stew into bowls. The emotion of the moment made him uncomfortable. He knew he had limited time left with his father and after having lost his mother years earlier he dreaded the day that he'd be completely alone in the world. His dad had been the most important person in his life for so long. They'd done everything together over the years — fishing trips, football games, even a half-marathon once when he was much younger. But those days were behind them, and all he wished was that he could go back in time and appreciate those moments one more time.

They ate together watching the Friday night rugby league game, exclaiming over dropped passes and rough play. Shouting when their team scored a try. Then, Franklin helped his father get ready for bed, kissed him goodnight, and walked back to his car through the darkened hallways and across the moonlit carpark, the empty Tupperware container in his hands. Loneliness descended on his soul once more and as he climbed into the car, he leaned his head back on the seat, eyes squeezed shut, and imagined for a single moment that he could find a way to another life — a life filled with love, laughter, and joy.

CHAPTER 6

MEG

*P*otato chip crumbs dotted the coffee table. Meg Taylor sighed, reached for the half-empty bag on the couch and folded over the top as she walked to the kitchen to put it away. She retrieved the wet cloth from the tap over the sink and returned to the small living room at the front of their cosy unit to wipe up the crumbs.

That was when she saw Brad's white sports shoes, socks stuffed into them, behind the table. Her lips pursed as she bent over to pick up the shoes. With a grunt she pushed herself back to her feet with one hand pressed to the coffee table. It wasn't as if her stomach was big yet, but she already felt a little off balance at sixteen weeks pregnant. She could only imagine how much worse that would get once her stomach grew larger.

She carried the shoes to their small bedroom and

stowed them in the closet behind the single sliding door. Clothes were strewn across the floor on Brad's side of the bed. She picked them up one by one and carried them to the hamper or lay them on the chair by the closet door, depending on how dirty they seemed.

Brad's paralysis was from the waist down. She had to fight the urge to snap at him over the amount of mess he left for her to clean up, given the fact that he was capable of doing so much more.

The problem was, he didn't think about it. Didn't consider how much extra work he made for her throughout the day. She'd already taken on massaging his tired muscles each evening, helping him get dressed and into and out of his chair, making his meals, packing the lunch he needed to take to university with him. There was so much on her plate that sometimes she wondered how on earth she'd manage to care for a baby as well.

She poked her head through the bathroom door, steam rushed at her face, she switched on the overhead exhaust.

"Everything okay in here?" she asked.

"Yeah, just enjoying the water," replied Brad.

She smiled. "Okay, well let me know when you need me."

The fact that he was able to enjoy having a shower on his own now was something of an accomplishment. He'd been angry about being unable to stand under the shower head, had refused to take up bathing in a tub, and had gone without bathing entirely for a while. At least now the anger over so much of what'd changed in his life had faded. He still flared up at times, but she could hardly blame him for that.

She tidied up a little more around the unit, then got to work packing Brad's lunch. She didn't bother packing much for herself other than snacks. Since about six weeks into her pregnancy, she'd switched from eating three meals a day to eating a dozen snacks. Her body looked decidedly rounder than it had a few months earlier, but it was the only way she managed to keep the nausea at bay for long enough to get everything done in her busy days.

The doctor had encouraged her that the nausea was likely to fade at twelve weeks or so, but that hadn't happened. She felt just as bad as she had in the middle of her first trimester. Still, she was otherwise in good health and was grateful for that. After all, as the doctor often reminded her, the pregnancy wouldn't last forever.

Just as she set Brad's lunch box on the end of the bench, he called her from the bedroom. She hurried to help him out of the shower into his chair, then to get dried off and dressed. She'd never imagined this is how her life would look as a newlywed, but one thing Meg had learned over the years was that life had a tendency to take you by surprise, and that feeling sorry for herself wouldn't help.

Besides, she often admonished herself, imagine how Brad felt. He was the one who'd suffered the life changing injury, had to give up his career on the international surfing championship circuit. The least she could do, as the woman who loved him, was to be there for him, to help with the small things.

Still, it was hard. Harder than she'd ever expected marriage to be. And she knew it was only going to get harder with a baby on the way. At first, she'd been ecstatic over the pregnancy, now that joy was tempered by the occasional bout of panic when she tried to imagine how she'd manage it all.

"Everything okay?" asked Brad.

She nodded. "Yeah, it's fine. I'm feeling a little bit stressed, that's all. I've got to get going, or I'll be late for work."

"The car should be here soon to pick me up for uni. Hey, I was thinking, we should look into getting one of those vehicles with the hand controls so I can drive myself around. We can't really afford to keep paying for a driver indefinitely, and we have that insurance payout."

Meg's lips pulled into a straight line. She nodded. "Hmmm." She wasn't so sure it'd be a good idea. After all, they didn't know how long that money would last, given the medical bills they had to repay, the ongoing physiotherapy, counselling and more.

"What does hmmm mean?" asked Brad, one eyebrow arching as she helped to pull a polo shirt over his head.

"It means, maybe."

"So you're in charge of all of the decisions now?" His voice was cold all of a sudden, his hazel eyes fixed on her face.

"No, of course not. Only, I'm thinking about that house we were talking about buying — for us and the baby. We need something bigger than this one-bedroom unit. Something with a backyard."

His eyes narrowed. "Well, I'm sure we can manage both. Don't you want me to be able to be more independent?"

"Of course I do."

"It doesn't seem like it," he said.

She sighed then straightened and tugged the front

of her shirt over the small bump growing beneath it. "It's not that. I'm anxious about how we're going to manage. You've still got almost four years of university left before you'll be an engineer. We've got medical bills, plus all of the costs of living, and a baby on the way. I think we should be frugal, that's all. I didn't say we shouldn't get the car, but I thought we wanted to look for a house first."

Brad's lips pursed. "And I'm telling you I think it'd be fine to get both a house and a new car."

"Okay." Irritation buzzed in her gut. When they'd dated, she'd never seen this side of Brad. She wasn't even sure he'd had this side to him before the accident. But, since his paralysis, he'd had moments where his words sliced like a knife.

"I don't think you really want me to be able to get around on my own."

Her eyes widened. "What? Of course I do."

"No, I think you like me depending on you."

She resisted the urge to stamp a foot as a swell of anger pushed up her spine. "No, I don't. I wish you were more independent. That'd make my life a whole lot easier. I'd love you to pick up after yourself for a start. Then I suppose we could talk about a car." Her heart fell as she heard the words tumbling from her mouth.

His eyes went cold. "Is that so? You're the mum and I'm the kid — pick up after yourself and you'll get a treat. Huh?"

He spun the chair away from her and wheeled out of the room. Meg pressed both hands to her face with a grimace. What was she thinking, talking to him like that? He'd been through so much, and for her to blame him was cruel in a way she'd hoped never to be.

Two tears trickled from her eyes and wandered down her cheeks as she slumped onto their bed. She heard the front door slam behind Brad as he left for uni, and a knot twisted in her gut.

THE SALON WAS BUSIER than usual that Friday. It was a long weekend and many of the women in town wanted their hair done for holiday celebrations with family and friends. She'd spent the morning staying out of people's way as much as possible, since it was hard to hide her melancholy. A few of the regulars had commented on her silence, but she'd brushed them off with a smile and a joke about pregnancy.

Meg finished sweeping a swathe of brown hair into a dustpan, then tossed it into the bin just as Vicky arrived. She'd forgotten her friend was coming in for her regular cut today, and her heart almost leapt from her chest at the sight of her round, beaming face.

"Vicky, it's so good to see you," she said, collapsing into her friend's arms.

Vicky held her a moment, stroking the back of her head, then stepped away to study her face. "You okay, hon?"

Meg dashed away a tear with the back of her hand. "Yeah, I'm fine. Just really happy to see a friendly face today."

"Okay." Vicky slipped an arm around Meg's waist as they walked side by side to the cutting chair. "I hope those hormones aren't wreaking too much havoc on you."

Meg shrugged. "I'm afraid they're turning me into a bit of a train wreck, but what can ya do?"

Vicky sat in the chair and Meg wrapped a cape around her. She set about combing Vicky's hair, then began to cut.

"I wish there was something you could do with my hair. It's so mousy, so straight — it really can't be styled." She sighed and her nose wrinkled.

"I think it looks lovely. Trust me, if you had these curls for a week, you'd be grateful for straight locks." Meg chuckled, tossing the red curls piled high on top of her head.

Meg's stomach curdled suddenly, nausea washing over her. She hadn't eaten in two hours since they'd been so busy tending to customers. And the longer she went between snacks, the worse her nausea became. She blanched and squeezed her eyes shut.

"What is it? What's wrong?" asked Vicky, turning in her chair.

Meg shook her head. "Nothing, just feeling sick all of a sudden. I forgot to eat."

"We should grab some lunch together. I haven't eaten either, and I'm dying to spend some more time with you. I've hardly seen you lately."

Meg smiled, working to keep the tears at bay. She'd been so much more emotional than she usually would, and Vicky's small kindness triggered an instant reaction. "That would be lovely. I'm almost finished here, so when I'm done, we can go. I've worked enough hours this week to take a long lunch, the boss won't mind."

She tidied up Vicky's haircut, quickly blew it out, then grabbed her purse from the staff room and met Vicky out front.

"Where should we go?" asked Vicky, running fingers through her soft, dark blond hair with a smile.

"How about Chinese food?" asked Meg. "I'm dying for some yum cha."

"Perfect," replied Vicky.

They headed to the *Chinese Garden*, found a table inside in the air conditioning, and sat across from each other. They didn't need menus; each of them knew exactly what they wanted to order, since it was the only Chinese restaurant in town.

For some reason, ever since she fell pregnant, all Meg wanted was salty and oily food. So, yum cha was a go-to lunchtime meal for her at least once per week.

Before long, the first tray of yum cha arrived, along with a pot of Chinese tea brought to them by a young woman with a blond ponytail who chewed gum and spoke in a monotone with a thick Polish accent.

Meg poured tea into both cups, then reached for a dim sum and took a bite, her eyes closing with delight as the flavours hit her tongue.

"Good?" asked Vicky with a laugh.

Meg nodded, but her mouth was too full to respond.

She swallowed. "It's the strangest thing — I feel so nauseated, like I'm going to throw up. But eating makes the feeling go away, at least temporarily. And I'm fine again, until my stomach is empty."

Vicky shook her head. "That is very weird. Whenever I feel like throwing up, food is the last thing I want to see or smell."

They chatted about Vicky's work as a vet, how things were going at the salon, and Sarah's surprise wedding while they ate.

"I can't believe she got married and didn't even tell us," opined Vicky with a shake of her head.

Although Meg wasn't surprised at all given Sarah's

private personality. Sarah had always been the quiet, determined type.

"And how about you?" asked Vicky, wiping her mouth with a napkin. "It seemed like you were upset about something when I arrived at the salon. Anything you want to talk about?"

Meg swallowed her bite of food and set her napkin down on the table next to her plate as emotions roiled inside. She wanted to talk to her friend about everything going on in her life, but that wasn't how she was raised. She and her siblings grew up in such tumult that they learned to keep everything bottled up, not to let anyone outside the family know what was going on inside the four walls of their rundown fibro house.

She inhaled a quick breath. "I'm worried."

"Worried about what?"

"What will happen when the baby comes." She met Vicky's gaze, then looked away, unwilling to allow the tears building in her throat to fill her eyes.

"Do you mean labour? Or something else?" asked Vicky, leaning forward in her chair, her face warm with compassion.

Meg's lips pursed. "Both. I mean, I'm worried about labour, of course. It's my first time, I don't really know what to expect. But there's more to it than that. Once the baby is here, what then? I'll have to work full-time, take care of the baby, take care of Brad... I don't know, I can't see how I'll manage."

Vicky shook her head. "That is a lot of pressure. I'm not sure you'll be able to do all of those things either. I don't think anyone could, at least not without help."

Hopelessness swamped her. Vicky was right — she couldn't do it. Why had she believed for a single moment that she could? She wasn't superwoman.

"I'm not trying to be unsupportive," offered Vicky, reaching for Meg's arm and squeezing it gently. "It's just that I think you're trying to take on too much, and it's not going to be healthy for you or your family."

Meg dropped her head into her hands. "I know. I know. I don't know what to do about it."

"Can Brad help more?"

Meg shook her head. "He's trying, of course he is, but I'm so ungrateful. It hasn't been that long really since his accident, and already I'm judging him in my head for not picking up his shoes and socks and putting them away or cleaning up after himself. It's hard, but I should be able to do those things for him without complaining. Shouldn't I?"

Vicky shrugged. "I don't know what you should or shouldn't be doing. But if something is upsetting you, then it's probably something you should both talk about."

"We did. I mean, we had a fight about it this morning. That's why I'm having such a terrible day." She groaned. "I should've kept my mouth shut, but now he's angry with me. We've been doing so well lately."

Vicky sighed. "I'm sorry. That's hard."

"Yeah, but I shouldn't complain. Should I? I have a husband who loves me, a job I enjoy, and a baby on the way. I should be happy, instead I'm sniping at my husband about crumbs on the coffee table. Ugh!" Her nostrils flared.

"I think you're being far too hard on yourself. You're allowed to have emotions, allowed to feel upset about everything. It's not fair what happened to Brad, but it happened to you as well. It's not fair to either of you, and you're both going to experience anger about that."

The tears Meg had been holding back welled in her eyes, blurring her vision. "When did you get to be so wise, Vicky Hawkins?"

Vicky laughed. "I don't know if I'm wise, but I definitely know how it feels to be angry about something and trying to hide it."

"You do?"

"Sure. I don't tell many people this, but my mum died when I was a teenager. It was a really hard time for me, losing her like that. But I was more worried about what it'd do to my sister and my little brother. So, I tried to be strong for them, to show them everything was going to be okay. The problem was, I didn't feel like anything would ever be okay again — in the end, I exploded and shouted at everyone, ran away, made some bad choices. But once I came back, I talked it through with my dad and my aunt, and I apologised to everyone. I felt much better, although the grief was still there. Still, I realised I didn't have to carry the burden alone, because there were people around me I could talk to about how I was feeling."

"Wow, I'm so sorry Vicky. I had no idea."

"I don't really talk about it much — I still keep it close to my chest. But every now and then I let someone see that pain, since it helps me to cope better by being open about it, and it helps them to see that there's hope things will get better. Anyway, it was a long time ago."

A lump filled Meg's throat. "That must've been so hard."

"It was. But I got through it. And you'll get through this as well."

Meg leaned forward to hug her friend over the table. "Thank you. Thank you for sharing that with me, and for your encouragement. I really needed that today."

"You're welcome." Vicky kissed her cheek. "And I think you're going to need some help after the baby comes."

"The problem is, I'm hopeless with money so I don't know if we have enough, or if I have to keep working. I wish I was close to my parents so I could talk to them about this stuff. I don't really know anyone I can get advice from about what to do."

"What does Brad think?" asked Vicky.

Meg resisted the urge to sniff. "I don't know. He says everything's going to be fine. But how can I believe that? I mean, it's clearly not going to be fine. There's just too much going on."

"Why does he think that?" asked Vicky.

"Because we got an insurance payout. He thinks it's enough to cover us until he can get a job after he finishes uni. But I don't know — that's a long time. I can't afford to give up my job at the salon. What if we lose everything and I'm desperate, and they've given the job away to someone else?"

A warm smile lit up Vicky's face. "Oh honey, sounds like you're carrying far too much fear around. Sometimes you just have to let go and trust. I've never been married, but my impression is that once you're married, you have to make these kinds of decisions together. But you're still trying to do it all alone."

Meg's heart dropped. Vicky was right. She hadn't considered following Brad's advice since she'd always had to make it on her own. Her parents had never helped her; she'd had to work from the moment she was old enough, and had moved to Emerald Cove to get away from her toxic family environment as soon as she'd saved enough money to manage it. All she'd done for as long as she could remember was fight for survival. She'd never considered letting go and trusting someone else.

"You think I should listen to Brad?"

"I'm not telling you what to do. But you love him, right?"

"Yes, of course."

"And before the accident, would you have trusted him to make sure the two of you were okay?"

Meg cocked her head to one side, imagining in her mind's eye the two of them walking down the beach, arm in arm, or eating at their favourite restaurant. They laughed a lot in those days. Had eyes only for each other.

"Yes," she admitted.

"Then maybe give him a chance to be right. And if all else fails, the three of you can live in my unit with me."

Meg laughed. "Now that sounds like a good plan."

Vicky squatted beside her, wrapped an arm around her shoulders. "There are plenty of people in your life who won't let you fall. You can't do life alone, sometimes you've just got to trust."

CHAPTER 7

BEN

*T*he Patrol's bonnet dipped, and the engine revved, a vicious roar that resounded loudly in the clay-filled hollow. The front tyres splashed into the muddy puddle at the bottom of the cut, and the vehicle halted temporarily, as though drawing a great breath before it pushed forward, levelling out as it crawled.

Ben Silver leaned over the steering wheel to peer through the mud-splattered windshield. He flicked on the wipers and a spray of water swept across the glass before being wiped away and leaving streaks of mud through his field of vision.

"So, how's work?" asked Leon, holding tight to the handle above the passenger window, his knuckles white.

Ben shrugged, steering the SUV over a series of

small boulders that led down to a slow-flowing muddy river. "It's okay, I guess."

"You're not loving it anymore?"

That was an understatement. The fact was, he'd been in his programming job for far too long. He was forty-four years old and should've moved into a management position long ago. But he'd liked the flexibility of being able to work from home, having time to do the things he loved like four-wheel driving and not having to be responsible for managing the inevitable office dramas.

"There's no satisfaction in it for me anymore. I guess it's time to look for something else."

"I can understand that," replied Leon. "Finance isn't exactly a party either."

Ben wouldn't swap jobs with Leon for a million dollars — he couldn't imagine anything more boring than filing tax returns. Although, these days, programming came close. It wasn't that he didn't love programming — he'd always loved it, both the logic and the mathematical language that came so easily to him and made everything straightforward. But he'd been doing it for so long, it was time to do something different.

"At least you got that promotion coming up. I don't have anything to look forward to."

Leon nodded. "That's true. It'll be good, I think. Unless I'm completely hopeless as a group manager, then it'll be a nightmare."

"You won't be hopeless. You'll kill it." Ben shot him a smile.

"And what are you gonna do?"

Ben let off the brake and pushed down slow on the accelerator to ease the vehicle into the river. Water rushed around the tyres, reaching to the top of the rims.

"Probably nothing. I should start putting out feelers, see what else is out there. The problem is, I'm not even sure I want to stay in the field — maybe I should try a completely different field. I've been doing the same thing for over twenty years."

"Yeah, you could take up interpretive dance — switch to wearing hemp pants and woven bracelets." Leon laughed.

"Sounds perfect." Ben grinned.

They made it through the river, and the SUV lurched up the bank on the other side, dripping water as they went. Gum trees lined the winding dirt track ahead of them, leaning over the road, shading it from the blazing sun overhead and sending patchy dappled light across their windshield.

As they moved away from the shallow river, the landscape became more arid, dry. The trees were replaced by squat shrubbery. Everything had a washed out, bleached look to it. In place of grass, most of the landscape was covered in a layer of reddish bull dust.

On the side of the road, something moved. Ben's gaze focused on the movement, anticipating an animal bounding into their path, and readying his foot on the brakes. As they drew closer, he saw the creature, but it wasn't moving now. It lay on the side of the road, still.

"What's that?"

Leon scratched his head. "What?"

"Over there, I saw something."

He pulled the vehicle to the side of the road and climbed out.

It was a wallaby. A small one. Something had

attacked it; pieces of flesh hung loose from its side and its tail was streaked red.

Leon followed him. "It looks in bad shape."

Ben grunted in response and squatted beside the wallaby. It struggled in place, as if to try and get away from him, then gave up when it was unable to move far and lay still again.

"Poor thing. Something's gotten a hold of it," said Leon.

Ben studied the wounds. "I think it's got a chance if we can take it to the animal hospital in time."

He tugged his T-shirt over his head and wrapped the wallaby up in it. The animal resisted at first, but as soon as it was wrapped snug in the shirt, it relaxed and allowed him to carry it back to the Patrol with him. He set the animal in his lap and tossed the keys to Leon who caught them with a grin.

"Really? I can drive?"

"Just don't get us stuck in a ditch."

It took longer at the animal hospital than Ben had thought it would. He'd intended to get home to work on a piece of code that'd been troubling the team for days, but he was running late. The veterinarian at the hospital wanted him to fill out a pile of paperwork about the wallaby, then he had to answer a series of questions and hang around while they ran tests to determine what was wrong.

Finally, they took the wallaby into surgery. Ben stroked its small, pointed face one last time, told it goodbye, and watched as they wheeled it from the room. He strode to his car, just as his mobile phone buzzed in his pocket.

"Hello, this is Ben."

"Hi, Ben it's Arthur. How are you?"

"I'm great thanks, Arthur. You?" Arthur was Ben's boss, but he hardly ever heard from him directly. Most of the time he worked with Project Managers, and only spoke to Arthur about KPIs and performance appraisals. Ben wondered what had prompted the call.

"I'm fine. Listen, I wanted to talk to you about your performance lately. I've spoken to the project leads you're working with, and they say your attendance is still sporadic. Remember, we spoke about that at our last meeting?"

Ben blinked. "Uh, yeah. Well, I had an emergency crop up today."

"Really?"

"Yeah, a wallaby on the side of the road…"

"Ben, I think it's time we parted ways. We've tried to make this work. But what we're really looking for in this role is someone who'll go above and beyond. Normally I'd have this conversation in person, but I'm in Singapore and I can't get back in time."

Ben scrubbed a hand over his eyes. "I understand."

The conversation was brief, to the point. Ben was out of a job. And he didn't blame Arthur, or anyone else there for that matter. He knew he'd been less than enthusiastic for a long time. His heart wasn't in it anymore. He should've left the role a long time ago. The only problem was, he didn't know where to go or what to do next. He felt adrift for the first time in his adult life. He wasn't moored to anything, or anyone. He could go where he liked, do what he liked. He'd saved enough money and made good investments that meant he didn't have to work if he'd rather not. Now, he had to figure out what he wanted to do with the next phase of his life, and the thought of it had his heart thudding against his ribcage.

* * *

THREE DAYS LATER, Ben had made his choice. He packed up his unit, gave the keys to a real estate agent to sell on his behalf, climbed into his car and headed south to Brisbane. He needed to get his bearings, figure out his next move, and the best way to start was by visiting his parents.

They were his safe place. Even though he was over forty years of age, he knew he would find a sympathetic ear and some wisdom from them. And besides, he hadn't seen as much of them lately as he would've liked. He'd spent weeks in Emerald Cove with Diana, the woman he'd recently discovered was his birth mother.

His adoptive parents were getting on in years, and he knew he wouldn't have them forever. In fact, being fired was probably the best thing for him at this point in his life — it would give him a chance to prioritise time with family.

He'd pondered the idea of moving to the Cove short-term to get to know Diana and his biological father, Andy, better. Maybe this was his chance to do that. It'd been jarring to meet Diana the first time — she looked so much like him, or rather he looked like her. And as he spent time with her, he'd discovered they had more in common than their looks. It was like finding out where he belonged — a feeling he'd never fully embraced before. It could be good to spend more time in the Cove and explore his past further. Perhaps he shared traits with Andy too. Time with them could unlock clues to some of the ways he'd always felt out of place in his life.

Or maybe he was just having a mid-life crisis. He'd heard about those, of course. But never expected that he'd go through one himself. Perhaps he should upgrade the four-wheel drive to a sports car and be done with it. He shook his head as he drove the vehicle along the highway. No, he didn't want a sports car, he only wanted to get to know his family better — and that now included biological parents who, until recently, had been complete strangers to him.

He turned off the highway, made his way through the suburbs to Chapel Hill and parked in the steep driveway of his parents' home. He'd grown up there, spent his young adult years living in the basement with its own kitchenette and sitting area. The sight of the seventies-style timber home warmed his heart. He trudged up the driveway, put his key in the lock and turned it, smiling at the sound of tiny toenails scrambling across the tiles.

Reaching down to pat the two small white dogs that threw themselves at his legs, keening furiously, he called out. "Mum, Dad, I'm home!"

CHAPTER 8

REBECCA

*T*he squat red brick building was a welcome sight. Rebecca climbed out of her car with a grin, tented a hand across her eyes and took it in for a minute. She was back.

She reached for her lunch box and water bottle on the passenger seat, then locked the car behind her as she sauntered across the parking lot and into the Emerald Cove police station.

"Well, if it isn't Miss Becky De Vries!" exclaimed Steph from behind a panel of bullet proof glass.

She buzzed Rebecca through, then enveloped her in a warm embrace, her eyes glistening. "It's so good to have you back."

"It's good to be back."

"So, I hear they made it permanent?"

Rebecca nodded. "Provisionally. I met with the big boss in Sydney. It's official — I can stay, at least for now. Which means they can back out if they want to anytime over the next six months, but I'm not too worried. I think I'll be able to prove myself in that time. At least I hope I can."

Steph's lips pursed. "Of course you will. The boss will be glad to see you, he's been moping around like a bear with a sore head ever since you left."

Rebecca's eyebrows arched. "He has?"

Steph winked. "But don't say I told you."

"Your secret's safe."

Rebecca headed down the short hallway, through the security door to the office beyond. Her desk was close to the door, so she reached it without running into anyone, and offloaded her purse and lunch. She flicked on the computer, but Franklin called her name from his office before the screen came to life.

Her stomach twisting with nerves, she smoothed her hair back and strode through the open office to see him. She hadn't run into him in weeks. They'd spoken on the phone a few times, but it felt like the first day of school after summer holidays. Why should she be nervous? It was only Franklin. Granted, she'd fantasised a few times about the two of them becoming more than just friends and partners, or boss and employee. But he didn't see her as anything more, and that was for the best.

A romance would ruin their professional relationship, and to tell the truth, she couldn't afford to lose a friendship or jeopardise her job now that she finally had one she loved and with some permanency.

"You're back," said Franklin as she walked through the door of his office.

He glanced at her from beneath lowered brows, then returned his focus to his computer screen.

"Yep, I'm ready to go to work again," she replied.

"We'll see."

Her brow furrowed. What did he mean by that? "You're not going to tie me to my desk, Sarge — surely?"

He grunted. "You'll do what you're told, Proby. I've got reports for you to file." He waved a hand at a pile of paperwork on one corner of his desk. "And after that, the filing room needs tidying."

"What? I—"

"What's that? You going to be insubordinate on your first day back, huh?"

Her hackles rose but she shut her mouth, jaw clenching tight. "No, sir," she said through her teeth.

"Good, welcome back. Get to it. We've got a staff meeting in half an hour."

Rebecca scooped up the pile of reports for filing and stormed from Franklin's office. After everything they'd been through, all she'd been through, he couldn't offer a few kind words of encouragement? She'd never understand that man, or the way his mind worked. She thought they'd gotten past this stage in their relationship to something more like a friendship, or at least mutual respect. Perhaps she'd been wrong.

As she sat in the file room, sliding reports into filing cabinets, her mobile phone rang.

"Good morning, this is Rebecca."

"Rebecca, it's Cameron Bueller, the administrative officer in Sydney assigned to monitor the Jake Hammond case. Is this a good time to talk?"

Her heart set up a staccato beat. "Yes, this is a good time."

"I thought you might like an update."

"That would be great," replied Rebecca, chewing on a fingernail, her eyes wide.

"Jake Hammond has been sentenced to ten years without the possibility of parole."

She jumped to her feet, a smile broadening her face. "Really? Ten years, that's great!"

"I thought you would be pleased."

She hung up the phone, still beaming, glanced around the room, an intense desire to tell someone about the phone call. She was alone in the file room, so rushed out to see Steph at the reception counter. Steph looked up from typing as soon as Rebecca approached.

"Bec, what is it?"

"Ten years, he got ten years!" Her vision blurred with tears.

Steph jumped to her feet, and the two of them danced in a circle, jumping up and down as Steph yelped with joy.

"That's so amazing! I'm proud of you." She pulled Rebecca into a bear hug. "You did good, sweetheart."

"Thanks." Rebecca wiped her eyes, hugged herself. She'd have to call her mother and Beth and tell them the good news. Now everyone could relax. Jake was going away for a long time, so she could live her life and forget all about him. At least for the next ten years. And who knew what might happen in that time — perhaps he'd change, maybe he'd move on and forget about her. Anything was possible.

"Did you tell the boss yet?"

"Not yet."

Steph grinned. "Go on, you should. He'll be stoked. I'm sure his testimony helped put Jake away as well as yours."

"I know it did. I'm so grateful to him, but I'm not

sure he cares as much as… well as much as I thought he did."

Steph's brow creased, she sat back in her seat to study Rebecca's face. "What do you mean by that?"

"I don't know, he wasn't exactly happy to see me this morning. He's done nothing but snap at me. Seems like he's angry with me. Or maybe he doesn't care about me as much as I thought he did, you know, as a partner, a friend."

Steph huffed. "Now, I know that's not true. He's been an absolute pain in the rear without you around."

"Maybe it had nothing to do with me, because he certainly didn't seem glad to see me."

Steph's frown deepened. "That's so strange. I'm sorry, love. I guess I was wrong."

"That's okay. I'll talk to him in a little while about the case, right now I just want to enjoy the moment a little longer. I might call Mum and tell her."

"Good idea. You deserve this, now you can finally get some peace."

She hurried back to her desk, called her mother, and relayed the happy news. Her mother was over-joyed. She cried and sniffled into the phone for ten minutes, until finally Rebecca said that she had to get some work done. She'd call Beth later that night. If she didn't get the filing done she'd never hear the end of it from Franklin.

Later, with the last file in her hand her knees were almost numb from kneeling on the hard, carpeted floor. Franklin pushed the filing room door open and poked his head through the gap.

"You done with the filing, Proby?"

She stood to her feet, stifling a groan as the feeling rushed back into her feet and knees. "Yep, done boss."

"Good, come with me. We've got a shoplifting case down at Hardy's."

She grinned. He was letting her out of the office. Maybe she wouldn't be confined to desk duty after all. "Well, let's go then."

* * *

THE CAR ENGINE lulled her spirit until the tension in her shoulders eased. Rebecca listened to the details of the case from Franklin, as much as he knew from dispatch, then settled in the driver's seat. If he was letting her drive, perhaps things weren't so bad between them as she'd thought. He hardly ever let her drive, and generally only if he had a lot to think about or was in a good mood.

She hoped it was the latter reason this time.

"So, I got an update on Jake's case from the Sydney office," she said, suddenly.

Franklin had one arm resting on the car's windowsill. He faced her with one eyebrow quirked. "Oh?"

"Yeah, he got ten years."

His lips pulled into a smile. "Really? That's good news, Proby. You must be happy about that."

"I am, it's what I'd hoped for. I mean, life would've been better, of course. But I'm happy with ten years."

"A lot can change in ten years."

"That's exactly what I told Mum."

He laughed. "I guess great minds think alike."

"I guess so." She met his gaze for a moment, and something sparked between them that made her heart skip a beat.

He cleared his throat. "So, I suppose this means you can put down roots, for a while anyway."

"Yeah, I'd like to do that."

"You think you'll stay here permanently, I mean, at least for now?"

"The Cove is my home."

"Really?" he eyed her, his expression unreadable. "I wasn't sure you'd want to. I mean, the brass approved you to be a Proby anywhere you wanted to go. They told me you'd likely pick a Sydney posting to be close to your family when I spoke to them."

"Did they? I don't know where they got that idea. I haven't said that. I want to stay here. I've built a life here. I have friends, a job, a terrible unit that stinks of fried food…"

Franklin laughed. "Okay, okay, I get it. I guess I thought you'd be leaving as soon as you got approval."

"Nope."

Now it all made sense. He'd thought she'd be leaving the Cove. But why had that made him transform into such a grouch? Or at the very least, more of a grouch than usual.

CHAPTER 9

FRANKLIN

The tension of the day had stirred up two big knots above Franklin's shoulder blades. As he drove home, he rested his head on one side, then the other, doing his best to work the tension from his muscles. He really needed a massage, but he wasn't the massage parlour type. The only time he'd ever received a massage in the past was from an ex-fiancée, who'd worked her magic on his neck and shoulders whenever he had a hard day. But that'd been years ago now, and he had no desire to revisit the past.

He pulled into the driveway, already going through the list of things he needed to do before he could put his feet up that night to watch the footy. He'd shopped the day before and had everything he needed to make spaghetti Bolognese for dinner. He'd take it over to the nursing home, then sit with his dad while they watched sports together. It was his favourite time of the day, although he couldn't help wishing they could be back in the comfort of their own home with his seventy-inch television screen.

Regardless of how tired he was, and how much he wished he didn't have to cook a meal and get in the car again, he couldn't keep the smile off his face. Bec was staying in the Cove. She'd told him as much. When the bigwigs in head office called to tell him she'd been approved to remain on the force, in a probationary capacity of course, they'd also mentioned they expected her to choose a location more suited to her — closer to her family. He'd been certain they were right, that they'd spoken to her and knew what she intended to do.

So, to hear from her own lips that she had no such desire lifted a giant weight from his shoulders that'd been pushing down on him for weeks. It was nothing more than a desire to keep the Proby he'd been working with for months — he had no wish to train someone new. Besides, he'd gotten used to her, and that was half of the battle when it came to working with a partner.

If the scent of her perfume made him feel a little heady, that was normal. He was a man, after all. And perhaps her smile lit him up inside, but it was a very good smile. Most likely she had the same effect on any man with a pulse. It didn't mean anything.

It was then he noticed the car parked on the curb. It was unfamiliar. Most likely someone visiting one of the neighbours. Someone from out of town — it was an expensive luxury vehicle, and he didn't know anyone in the area with the latest model Mercedes in white with gold trim.

He unlocked the door and stepped into the kitchen,

and something moved in the shadows by the refrigerator. He reached for his hip, hand covering the place where his gun should be — but he'd locked it up at the station overnight.

"Hello Frankie," came a soft, feminine voice.

He exhaled the breath he'd been holding. "Nicole Edwards, what are you doing in my kitchen?" His ex-fiancée, the woman who'd flashed through his mind only minutes earlier after years without so much as a thought about her. It must've been some kind of premonition — only he didn't believe in stuff like that, so more likely it was the oily burger he'd had for lunch, or the pounding headache that was working its way through his skull, or merely a coincidence.

She laughed and stepped into the light. "I thought it was about time I visited my old friend."

"Friend?" he questioned, filling a glass with water, and downing it in one large gulp. "How did you get in? I should charge you with breaking and entering."

"You haven't changed your locks, honey. I knew you wouldn't have — you don't like change, never have." She stepped closer, a floral skirt swirling around her lithe, tanned legs, her blue eyes flashing beneath blond curls.

There were more lines around her eyes and in the curves of her smile, a few more freckles across her nose and on her arms, but otherwise she looked exactly the same as she had five years earlier when she broke off their engagement and walked out of his life without so much as a backwards glance.

He shrugged. "True. I should probably get those keys back."

She laughed, rested a hand on his shoulder. "Don't I get a hug?"

He embraced her, feeling her arms wind around his neck in a way that brought memories rushing in like storm clouds. Her body against his reminded him of old times; he stepped back, confusion clouding his already turbulent thoughts. The headache worked its way up to the top of his skull.

"You don't seem happy to see me," she said.

"It's been a long day, sorry if I'm not chirpy enough for you."

She shook her head, blue eyes dancing. "Ah, some things never change."

"Not around here, anyway," he added.

"I'm glad," she said, surprising him. "I'd hoped nothing would've changed and I can see it hasn't. The Cove looks exactly the same. So do you. Where's your dad?"

He sighed. "In a nursing home. He had a stroke a few months ago."

Her smile faded. "I'm sorry, I know how much you love him. That must be hard on you."

"It is." He combed a hand through his hair, setting it on end. She knew him so well; it felt good to have an old friend to talk to about his father. She remembered the good times they'd had together, how much fun his father had been. He didn't have to explain, she understood how he felt. No matter what else had happened between them, they'd always have the tug of a first love linking their hearts.

"In fact, I'm about to make dinner then go see him to watch the footy, so…"

"I'll join you," she said, her smile brightening. "It'll be like old times."

His lips pursed. He'd intended to make his excuses or tell her he'd see her another time, but she seemed to have no intention of leaving, and he knew her well enough to know that she'd get her way no matter how he felt about it.

"Fine, you can cut the onion then," he said.

Her nose wrinkled. "Still can't stand it, huh?"

He grunted. "Makes me cry every time."

She laughed, throwing her head back so that the curls danced around her tanned shoulders.

* * *

CINDY

The scent of mineral powder filled Cindy's nostrils as she dabbed the brush one last time against her cheeks. With a grimace, she pulled the hair back from her face, noting the wrinkles around her blue eyes and the lines that made furrows on the edges of her mouth where her lips curled into a smile. Laugh lines, they were called. At least she'd earned those ones: she wouldn't swap them for smooth skin. Not a chance. She'd relish every single moment of laughter in her life, all the times she'd bounced babies on her knees, special moments when they'd sat around the dinner table sharing funny tales about their days, or even when she'd laughed at herself over something silly she'd done.

"So, is this a date?" asked Sarah, smoothing the covers on Cindy's king-sized bed before sitting down.

Sarah's brown hair fell on both sides of a smooth part over each of her tanned shoulders. She grinned, her eyes sparkling.

Cindy shrugged. "I suppose you could call it that.

71

Although, I'm sixty-one years old, so I don't really think about it that way."

"It's definitely a date," replied Sarah, still grinning. "Who would've thought, you and Doctor Dreamy."

"He's hardly Doctor Dreamy. He's a reputable professional, who happens to have been a good friend to this family for many years."

"And he's so very dreamy," added Sarah, fluttering her eyelashes.

Cindy couldn't help laughing at the expression on her daughter's face. She kissed her on the cheek, then sat beside her on the bed.

"I don't know. It's so strange to be dating again at my age. I never would've imagined myself doing this. But then again, a lot of things have happened over the past couple of years that I didn't see coming."

Sarah leaned her head on Cindy's shoulder. "I'll admit, it is a little odd to help my mother get dressed for a date."

Cindy chuckled. "Thanks."

"But I want to see you happy, and Dr Miller seems to make you happy."

"You know, you should probably start calling him Athol."

Sarah's nose wrinkled. "Hmmm. I suppose I can try. Although he's been Dr Miller for my entire life, so that's going to be hard to change."

"Well, thanks for trying anyway. And thanks for being here. Athol and I have been seeing each other for a few weeks now, but this is the first time we'll be out in public together. I only hope the entire town isn't watching."

"Oh they'll definitely be watching," replied Sarah, standing and using her fingers to fix her mother's grey-blond curls. "But you shouldn't worry about that. They'll find out about the two of you soon enough. So, it might as well be tonight."

Cindy cupped Sarah's cheek in the palm of her hand. "What did I do to deserve such a good daughter?"

Sarah shrugged. "I've neglected you for a lot of years. It was time I came home and took care of you."

"I'm not that old, am I?" asked Cindy, holding a necklace up in the mirror on her dressing table to see if it suited the aqua dress she was wearing.

"You'll never be old to me." Sarah embraced her, squeezed tight then released her. "Anyway, I've got to get going. Heaps of work to do. Have a good time tonight, and you kids be good. Okay?"

* * *

CINDY FOLDED the menu and set it on the table beside the place setting. A white napkin, folded into the shape of a boat, or hat or something else she couldn't quite identify, sat on top of a white china plate.

Athol ordered a bottle of wine, then focused his attention on her. His brown eyes sparkled. "I'm so glad we're finally doing this. I've been wanting to take you out to eat at a nice restaurant for ages. This is one of my favourite places."

"I can't wait. I've never eaten here before, and I love Italian food."

The restaurant, *Ciro's*, was located in Burleigh Heads close enough to the beach to smell the salt in the air, but far enough away that she had to squint to see the waves curling to shore through a line of tall casuarinas, their branches full of plump green needles.

"I'm glad, Italian is the best food in the world in my humble opinion."

"Well, I love to cook it. I'll have to make it for you sometime. The kids have always bragged about my lasagna. My chicken carbonara as well."

"That sounds amazing." He reached for her hand across the table and rested his on top of hers.

A spark of attraction flitted through her, unsettling her in a way she hadn't expected. They'd spent a good deal of time together in recent weeks, although she'd told Athol she wanted to take things slowly. He'd assured her he understood. Although sometimes it seemed to her he wanted to move things along more rapidly than she was ready for.

As if reading her thoughts, he spoke. "Do you remember how we said we'd take things slowly?"

She nodded. "Of course."

"Do you still feel the same way?"

Cindy cocked her head to one side, studied the man seated in front of her. If she was honest with herself, and with him, she'd lost faith in her ability to judge character after everything Andy had put her through. Had she been too blind to see what he was doing? How had she failed to recognise all of the ways, big and small, he'd overlooked her, mistreated her, taken her for granted?

But this man was a good man. Everything inside her whispered that Athol was kind, considerate, thoughtful, selfless — he was a doctor after all, the kind of man who'd spent his life putting the needs of others ahead of his own. And yet, could she trust him? Could she trust herself to choose wisely when it came to matters of the heart?

The waitress set their food in front of them, topped up their wine glasses and left with a nod.

Before she could respond to Athol's question, he continued. "Because I want you to know I only said that to ease your mind." He squeezed her hand. "I've known you my whole life, Cindy Flannigan, and it's been some years now since I've grown to love you."

Her heart skipped a beat. She'd never considered the man across from her had developed feelings for her. All of those family BBQs he'd attended after his wife died, all of the Christmases he'd spent with them, the trips to the beach where they'd laughed over games of cricket or frisbee. He'd been a good friend to her, to their family. But she'd considered him Andy's friend more than anything. They'd always been there for each other, Andy and Athol, the best of friends who'd do anything for the other.

And yet, they'd fallen out of touch after Andy left Cindy. Athol didn't approve of the way his friend had treated his wife of almost forty years. And Cindy had to admit that his anger with Andy was part of the attraction. She hadn't expected to find loyalty in Andy's closest friend, yet that's exactly what he'd given her.

"I don't know what to say."

"It's okay, you don't have to say anything. I know I've sprung this on you, and you'll need some time to think about it. But I wanted you to know, I love you. I've loved you as a friend for as long as I can remember, and that love developed into something more in the past few years when I saw how alone you'd become in your marriage, how Andy didn't respect you or treat you the way you deserve to be treated, and the way you showed him grace in your response."

A wellspring of emotion swirled in Cindy's gut. "You knew what was going on? Knew he was cheating on me?"

"No, not really," he replied. "I had my suspicions, and when I talked to him about it he always put me off. Told me not to worry about it, he had everything under control. Of course, now I know that wasn't true."

She wanted to love again, wanted to be able to open up, but it was difficult for her to trust. Athol was a good man; she knew that much. The comparison between his character and that of her ex-husband was stark. Still, the idea of letting someone into her heart gave her indigestion.

"I care about you, Athol. I care very much."

"I know." He smiled.

"So, let's see how things go."

"That sounds perfect."

"Can I change the subject?" she asked.

He laughed. "Of course."

"What do you think of me selling my house?"

His eyebrows arched high. "What? Would you really consider doing that?"

She shrugged. "Why not? It's too big for me and Petal to live in on our own. I'm getting too old to spend so much of my time cleaning and gardening. I want to do other things with my spare time. I've had enough of working my fingers to the bone." She sighed. "And there are so many memories lingering in every room."

"Good memories too," he added.

She dipped her head. "Good memories as well, of course."

"But what about the kids? What will they say?"

Her lips pursed. "They'll hate the idea. It's their childhood home, so of course they'll be upset if I sell. But I don't know what else to do. It's been so hard since Andy left, trying to manage the house and the cafe on my own."

"It's too much for one person," he agreed.

"So, I think I'm going to downsize."

He raised his glass. "To downsizing, and new chapters."

She grinned and raised her own glass to his. "I'll drink to that."

CHAPTER 10

CINDY

"What do you mean you're selling the house?" shouted Sarah from the kitchen.

In the office, Cindy grimaced. This was always going to be difficult, but she had to face her children sometime. She figured it would be best to start with Sarah, they'd always had a close bond and her eldest usually came around without the need for too much angst.

Cindy carried a box of folders and pens out to the living room and set it on top of another box she'd packed from the office. "Just what I said. I'm selling to downsize."

"But this is our home. We've lived here my whole life," objected Sarah, striding into the living room with both hands cupping a mug of hot tea.

"Actually, you live somewhere else if you'll recall."

Cindy grinned, shaking her head. "You're all adults and I live alone in this big, draughty old place. It's not simply that I feel lonely, banging about in here, but it's too much for me to maintain on my own."

"Does Dad know?" asked Sarah.

Cindy's gut twisted into a knot. The last thing she wanted to do was talk to her ex-husband about her personal life. They were divorced, she'd gotten the house in the settlement. In fact, she'd been the one to pay it off, so she hardly thought she owed him anything, let alone insight into her life choices.

"No, I haven't told him. Haven't seen him, other than a brief encounter in the street outside Foodstore."

"Oh, you saw him shopping?"

Cindy nodded. "Him and Keisha. They're back in town, I guess."

"Yeah, I had dinner with them a couple of nights ago. Sorry, Mum, I should've told you."

Cindy hated the idea of her children eating family meals with Andy and Keisha, while she sat home with Petal, eating leftovers, and watching reruns of *The Bachelor*.

"That's okay. I'm glad you and your dad are reconnecting. But I'm not going to talk to him about selling the house. It's my house, I'll sell it if I want to." She pushed out her chin and marched back to the office to fetch another box.

There was no need for her to begin packing since she hadn't listed the house for sale yet. But it had a large basement, and she figured it wouldn't hurt to pack as many things into boxes as possible and store them in the basement before listing so the house didn't look cluttered; it would help her move more quickly when the time came.

Sarah followed her into the office, picked up an empty box, and stacked books from the bookshelf into it, one at a time. "You're right, Mum. You can sell the place if you want. Maybe it's for the best. I do worry about you here all alone — and you work too hard as well."

Cindy sighed. "Thank you. I need you to back me up; sometimes I feel as though I'm an island — especially when you kids all gang up on me over something. That was one of the good things about your father, he never let the three of you push me around too much and always stepped in if I got overwhelmed."

"Wow, you're complimenting Dad?" Sarah's eyebrows quirked.

Cindy shrugged. "He has a lot of good qualities. I'm not going to pretend otherwise. I wouldn't have married him if he didn't."

"So, where will you move?" asked Sarah, reaching for a Sharpie to mark the box.

"I'd like to be near the water. But something small, without too many stairs."

"I'm sure you'll be able to find something like that in Emerald Cove. There are plenty of cottages along the waterfront."

"I'm meeting an agent now, actually. Would you like to come along?"

Sarah gaped. "What? Already? But—"

"I want to look around, see if there's anything that fits my needs before I list this place. I might hate all of them and decide not to move, after all." Cindy finished packing a box of stationery supplies and taped it shut in one deft move.

She and Sarah carried their boxes out to the living room and stacked them up.

"Okay, I'll come with you if you don't mind me tagging along."

"I'd love you to come."

* * *

THE CHALET STYLE house had a triangular entryway. It looked as though it'd been built in the nineteen seventies, but it had been updated and painted since then. The white trim was accented with navy blue shutters and a navy roof that stood in contrast to the pale shrubbery around the front of the house and the cottage garden spotted with white flowers and dark green climbing vines on weather-worn trellises.

"What do you think?" Sarah chewed on a fingernail, squinting up at the house.

"It's got a lot of character, which I like. And this location is perfect."

Cindy spun on her heel to take in the view. The street was called Cliffside Drive, and it ran along the beach in front of the chalet, then curved away from the water and up a steep incline topping a cliff that looked out over the ocean.

"It's beautiful. I could definitely imagine you taking walks on that beach and drinking tea on the front verandah as you watch the sun rise."

Cindy let her eyes drift shut as the fresh, salty air filled her lungs. "I feel more relaxed already."

"So do I. I have to admit, I'm coming around to your way of thinking. I can see why you'd rather live somewhere like this," said Sarah.

"Besides the fact my house is too big, and too much upkeep, Di moved away as well. So, it doesn't feel the same there anymore. Ethan has his own place now;

while he was staying with me it felt like old times but now…"

"I get it. Let's go and have a look inside, see if this place is as cute as it seems."

They walked around the house. It had two stories, but the main bedroom and bathroom were on the ground floor, which suited Cindy perfectly. The only rooms upstairs would be guest bedrooms and a rumpus room, so it would be perfect for when family and friends visited. The more she saw, the more Cindy loved the house. It was only the third house the agent had shown them that afternoon, but she was already in love with it.

By the time they climbed into her car and headed for home, Cindy had made up her mind.

"That's the house for me," she said.

Sarah nodded. "I think it's great. Now, you just have to sell your place."

For the first time, Cindy felt ready to sell the home where she'd raised her family and move on to the next phase of her life. The chalet on Cliffside Drive would be the perfect place to do just that.

CHAPTER 11

REBECCA

*T*he sun rose over the glittering water, making it appear silver. Small waves rose and crashed against the dark shoreline as Rebecca ran in the wet sand. Her feet dug deep, leaving a trail in her wake that showed her stride had lengthened, her strength and stamina returning after her run-in with Jake. She felt good — better than she had in years.

She grinned when she spotted the fish and chips shop with her small unit above it, changed course, and aimed up the beach, through the thick, dry sand that pulled at her, making her puff harder.

Sweat dripped down both sides of her face and trickled down the length of her spine.

As she reached the road, she stopped to let a car pass. A taxi pulled up in front of the restaurant and she tented a hand over her eyes to block out the glare as she studied it.

Who was that getting out of the cab? It looked like her mother, but that couldn't be, since she was in Sydney.

Her heart skipped a beat. She sprinted across the road with a shout.

"Mum! What are you doing here?" Rebecca threw her arms around her mother and squeezed. "Sorry, I'm all sweaty and gross."

Mum laughed and stepped back to reach for her suitcase as the taxi driver wheeled it over. She paid the man and followed Rebecca to the unit upstairs.

"I didn't have anything to do this weekend, and I thought — what I really wanted to do was to visit you. Since I can do it now, and for years I couldn't, there was no stopping me." She laughed. "Aren't you glad to see me?"

Tears clogged Rebecca's throat as she unlocked the door and pushed it open. "I'm so happy I could cry." She kissed her mother's cheek as they passed through the opening. Then she shut the door behind them.

"I'm glad. I wanted to surprise you."

"Well, you did. My heart is still pounding." Rebecca pressed a hand to her chest. "The only thing is, well, I have to work today."

"Oh, that's fine, love. I know you have things going on. You just go about your day as if I'm not here. We can spend time together tonight."

Rebecca nodded, filled a glass with water from the kitchen tap and gulped it down.

"I'm going to take a shower. Can I make you a cup of tea?"

"I'll get that, love. You have your shower, and don't worry about me. I know my way around."

Rebecca smiled. "Hey, why don't you come to the

station with me? I know everyone would love to meet you. And it'd give you a chance to see where I work."

"That sounds delightful. I can't wait to see Franklin again. The last time he was here, we had that dinner at the Chinese restaurant together, and he was such a gentleman. It seemed to me there was something of a spark between the two of you." Mum's eyes twinkled. She pushed down the handle on her luggage and lay it on the floor against the wall.

Rebecca's face flushed with warmth. "I don't know about a spark. Sometimes I think it might be nice to see where things could go between us, but I don't know."

"What don't you know?"

"If he feels the same way. He sees me as an employee, maybe even a friend, but nothing more than that." She sighed and tugged the hairband from her ponytail, letting her dark brown hair cascade around her shoulders.

"Well, from what I saw, he seemed very keen on you. But maybe I was wrong." Mum arched an eyebrow.

"Maybe, I suppose we'll see. But he's very difficult to read."

"Well, you're not exactly an open book yourself."

* * *

REBECCA SHOWED her mother around the station, introduced her to the team, and took her to the kitchen to fix them both a cup of coffee before the morning meeting. She was proud of her workplace, excited to show her mother where she went each day and to show her off to the team as well.

Her life seemed entirely changed from what it'd been. It was as though a light had been switched on, pushing out the darkness she'd walked in for so many years. She was happy. It was hard for her to believe, but there it was. She was excited about the future and felt hope that things would be okay.

"Everyone is lovely and they all seem crazy about you," said Mum, sipping her coffee.

Rebecca grinned. "Well, I'm pretty loveable."

Mum's nose wrinkled. "That is true. Of course, you got that from me."

They were both laughing when Franklin walked into the kitchen followed by a leggy blonde in a tiny pair of shorts and a clinging satin top.

"Franklin!" chimed Mum. "There you are, Bec has been showing me around your wonderful office."

Franklin smiled and embraced her. "It's so good to see you again, Liz. I didn't know you were coming to town."

"It was a surprise," replied Mum, glancing lovingly at Rebecca.

"I'm sure Bec is very happy to have you back." His gaze met Rebecca's and she crossed her arms over her chest, smiling shyly. Her voice stuck in her throat — what she wanted to say was, who's the girl? Instead, she stood in silence, watching as Franklin poured coffee for the two of them, the woman's hand resting on his shoulder.

Mum exchanged a look with Rebecca, one eyebrow quirked in a question that she didn't have an answer for. She shrugged in response.

"Well, I suppose we'll see you later, Franklin," said Mum.

He nodded, smiled. "Yes, of course. See you later, Liz. See you at the meeting, Proby."

Rebecca offered him a curt nod of the head, then followed her mother from the kitchen. Who was that? And why did she have her hand on his shoulder? She had so many questions and no answers. No, that wasn't entirely correct. She had one answer to a question her mother had asked her — it was clear Franklin wasn't interested in Rebecca as anything more than a partner, and she'd been imagining things all along.

MEG

The last few steps to the unit's front door left Meg puffing hard. She leaned against the door while searching in her purse for the keys. Dark clouds whipped across the sky, covering the sun, and making the afternoon look as though it was evening. Finally, she found the key, pushed it into the lock, and turned.

The unit was bathed in a dull gloaming. Where was Brad? He should've been home from uni an hour ago. She'd had to work later at the salon then she'd wanted to because a client came in who wanted Meg to colour her hair and no one else would do.

With one hand resting on her burgeoning stomach, Meg gulped great mouthfuls of water from a glass, standing in the middle of the kitchen. Her legs ached, her feet hurt, and all she wanted to do was to sit. But, for now, she had to get ready to go to an appointment.

She grabbed an apple and crunched on it, the sweet and tart flavour bursting across her tongue as she hurried to her bedroom to freshen up.

Within five minutes she was seated in the living room, her purse in her lap, one foot tapping on the carpeted floor.

He still wasn't home.

Finally, a car door slammed outside the block of units. She stood, pushed through the front door, and locked it behind her. Brad wheeled himself up the footpath as the car he'd taken drove off behind him.

Her lips pursed. She didn't want to give him a hard time about it, but they'd be late. The appointment was important, her twenty-week scan, and he had promised to be home early so they could drive there together.

"I'm sorry I'm late," he said when he saw her.

She nodded. "Let's get going, we can talk in the car."

He followed her down the ramp to the parking garage and she helped him into his seat then stowed his chair in the back. When she slumped into the driver's seat, she held back tears — she was tired and had been working so hard for so long. All she wanted was some rest. How would they do this? Being a parent was difficult enough, but she had to carry so much of the load for both of them — could she manage it?

"I'm sorry," he said again, as she pulled the car onto the road.

She inhaled a quick breath. "I know. But Brad, you said you'd be home early. I could've gone without you, but you wanted to come, and now we'll be late."

"I have good news," he countered.

She offered him a wary glance. "Oh?"

"I got a job."

"What?" Her pulse quickened.

"Well, it's an unpaid internship really. But still, it's a start."

Her spirits slumped. "Oh. That's great, honey."

He reached over to massage the back of her neck. "I know it's not going to help with money right now, but it's a good way to get in the door. I'm still studying, but maybe they'll give me a paid job after I graduate."

She smiled. "I think it's wonderful. I'm proud of you."

"Thanks," he replied. "Of course, it's going to mean I'm away more."

"I know." Meg studied the road ahead of her, unwilling to say more.

"We're going to be okay. Everything will work out. You worry too much."

One eyebrow quirked and she shook her head. "Do I?"

"Yes, you do. We have the insurance payout, so we'll manage for a while on that. Plus, your job…"

"But I'd really like to pull back at work. I'm so tired all the time."

"I think you should."

"But how will we…?"

"Meg, you're going to have to trust me. I've run the numbers, we can manage. I'd love for you to be able to stay home with the baby. And if I do well at uni, and my internship, I'll get a good job as soon as I graduate, and we'll be fine."

She wanted to believe him; some part of her knew he was right, but having grown up poor, there was always a drive inside to keep pushing, to plan for the worst, to make sure there was always money coming in. Even the thought of taking time off work sent a flash of panic through her chest, making her gulp for air. Her friends had encouraged her to trust Brad, so maybe she should.

"Okay," her voice was shaky. She reached for his hand and squeezed it, keeping her eyes on the road. "That sounds good."

"Perfect, so you'll take time off work when the baby comes?"

She swallowed then nodded. "I'll take time off."

"Good." He grinned, and she couldn't help smiling along with him. "It's going to be amazing. I can't wait to be a dad."

Her brow furrowed. "Really? I thought you were anxious about it."

"I am," he conceded. "But I've been thinking about it, and we can do this. It'll be hard, especially on you, but I really want to be a good dad — I want to do everything I can to take care of my family, to be there for both of you."

A lump formed in her throat. "You *will* be a good dad. I've always thought that about you. In fact, I have a feeling you'll be the favourite."

He laughed. "That's my plan."

They arrived at the medical imaging office ten minutes later than their appointment time, but when they'd checked in, they discovered the staff was running behind by half an hour. Meg sat in the waiting room, flicking through a magazine, as the tension of the day slowly eased from her shoulders.

Next to her, Brad had his backpack in his lap and his nose in a textbook. She was impressed with how quickly he'd dived into his studies, how seriously he took it. For someone who'd planned to spend a good portion of his life on the professional surfing circuit, who'd never really excelled academically before, he'd surprised her with how well he'd taken to studying engineering, and how much he seemed to enjoy it.

"Meg Taylor," called a woman with a dark ponytail, dressed in blue scrubs.

Meg and Brad followed the woman into a room, where she explained the procedure. Meg situated herself on the table, and the woman spread a cold jelly across her stomach, then began the scan. Meg's heartbeat thudded in her ears. She was nervous. They'd find out the sex of the baby today. Excitement sent a flicker of adrenaline through her veins.

Beside her, Brad sat in his chair, watching the screen with wide eyes, a grin tweaking the corners of his mouth.

"So, I'm going to check everything out, make sure the baby's healthy and everything's okay," said the woman, smiling as she manoeuvred the paddle across Meg's abdomen. The jelly was cold, and inside her the baby wriggled — like a butterfly's tickling wings.

They chatted while the woman worked, noting down measurements, and talking through what she was doing. Finally, she showed them the baby's beating heart and the sound of it brought tears to Meg's eyes.

"It looks like you're having a girl," the woman said.

Meg and Brad exchanged a look as Meg's vision blurred. "Wow, a girl."

Brad laughed. "I'm going to be outnumbered." He placed a hand on Meg's arm. "I'm so happy."

She was too. He'd been so down since his accident. To see the smile on his face now, hear him say he was happy — it was everything she wanted. They'd get through this; they'd be a family — one nothing like the one Meg had grown up a part of. She was going to be the kind of mother she'd always wished she'd had, and Brad would be a wonderful father.

The woman's brow furrowed. "Wait here a moment, I'll be right back."

She left the room, and Brad reached over to cup Meg's cheek where she lay.

"She's beautiful," he said.

Meg could only nod.

The woman came back into the room, this time with another woman wearing a long, white lab coat. They studied the screen together for a few moments, then the woman in the white coat sat on a chair opposite Brad and Meg while the other woman wiped the jelly from Meg's stomach. She introduced herself, her face expressionless.

"I want to talk to you about something we've found during your scan today."

Meg scooted upright, pulling her shirt down.

The doctor continued, telling them some of the measurements were off. She recommended additional testing to find out more, but it was possible their baby had abnormalities. She couldn't say for certain yet what the issue was, but there seemed to be something wrong with the length of the baby's legs, the size of her head. It could be something called lethal skeletal something or other. Meg wasn't sure what exactly came next, the impact of the doctor's words had stolen the breath from her lungs.

CHAPTER 12

FRANKLIN

"*I*t's just dinner," said Nicki.

Franklin scrubbed both hands over his face. He leaned his head to one side, holding the phone in place with his ear as he finished washing the dishes in the sink.

His kitchen was neat and tidy, the way he liked it. Clean dishes were stacked in rows on the drying rack. The cream-coloured benches were tidy and gleamed under warm lighting. He'd replaced them a year earlier but hadn't gotten around to replacing the dark brown tiles that lined the wall above the benches. The house was quiet and lonely these days without Dad around, but it was still his refuge; the place he went to rest and recover after a long day patrolling the Cove.

As much as he'd embraced the calm of coming home after work, had changed into basketball shorts and a T-shirt with a hole under one arm, and pulled a beer out of the fridge ready to crack open, he couldn't relax. His ex-fiancée wanted him to go to dinner with her, and that had his stomach twisting into knots. Why was she back in the Cove? He'd done everything he could to be polite and congenial; he'd chatted with her over coffee — catching up on old times was how she'd put it. When she asked to be shown around the station, he'd done it, even though he'd had to put up with all of the questioning glances, and the not-so-subtle questions from the team after she left.

Now she wanted to go to dinner, and if there was one thing he knew about Emerald Cove, it was that the two of them having dinner at one of the few restaurants open on a Monday night could only mean one thing — everyone would know about it by the end of the week and he wouldn't be able to escape the comments and questions from curious townsfolk.

Nicole Edwards had grown up in the Cove. Most people knew who she was and how their engagement had ended, and he could tell exactly what they thought of seeing the two of them together again by the disapproving looks on the faces of every person who happened upon them. Like when she'd followed him into Foodstore and walked around the entire supermarket with him chattering on about her new life in Hong Kong, how wonderful it was, and how much she'd loved singing at the nightclubs there for a nice, fat paycheck. They'd bumped into Marg at the deli counter, who'd forced a smile onto her face and announced in a high-pitched voice how lovely it was to see Nicole again after all this time — her tone indicating that it was in fact, the opposite of lovely in her opinion, as she shot a wide-eyed look in Franklin's direction beneath a blue curl that'd escaped from her hair net, and he did everything he could to avoid her gaze.

He sighed. "What are the chances of you leaving me alone if I agree to this?"

"Frankie, I can't believe you're talking to me like that. Don't you want to see me? After all, it's been years."

"I know exactly how long it's been since you walked out on me, don't worry about that." He cringed at the defensiveness that crept into his tone. The last thing he wanted to do was to let Nicole know how much she'd hurt him, to give her that power over him again.

She was the only person who called him Frankie. He hated the name.

"That's the thing. I want to have a chance to hash it all out, apologise for what I did. We have things we need to talk about, to get closure."

"Closure? I don't need closure. I'm perfectly fine leaving things wide open. In fact, I love it that way. Un-closed, that's the latest craze — if not, then I'm starting a new craze. I don't know why everyone's always going on and on about needing closure. Really, that's the last thing I need. Open, free, oblivious, blissfully ignorant, call it whatever you like, that's the way that suits me best." He grunted as if to punctuate his rant, letting the dirty water out of the sink and wiping his hands dry on a tea towel.

She ignored his words. Nothing new in that department. "Please, Frankie. Dinner, that's all. After that, I will leave you alone, if that's what you want."

He shook his head slowly. There was always more to it, but he didn't know how to squirm his way out of this one without coming across as a complete jerk. In the end, it came down to this — they'd grown up together, she was his first love, and he never could say no to her. "Okay, fine. We can have dinner at the Chinese Garden. But I don't want to be out too late, I've got work tomorrow."

"Don't worry, Grandpa," she said. "I'll tuck you in bed nice and early."

His lips pursed. What was he getting himself into? "I'll meet you there at eight."

"Perfect, see you then."

* * *

NICOLE'S blond curls bounced on her tanned shoulders as she talked, gesticulating to emphasise her words, tipping her head back to emit that deeply infectious laughter that'd always made him smile. Franklin leaned back in his chair to study her, the Chinese food cooling in dishes on the table in front of him.

She seemed thinner than she'd been the last time he saw her. And her clothes were more expensive. The five years they'd been apart had flown by for him — it felt like yesterday she'd walked out, leaving him broken-hearted.

"What do you think?" she asked.

He shook his head. "I don't know."

"You weren't listening, were you? I told you an entire story — a hilarious story if I do say so myself — and you didn't hear a word of it. Off in your own world again."

He shrugged. "What are you doing here?"

She sighed, rested her folded arms on the table. "I wanted to see you."

"And?"

"And, I'm considering moving back to the Cove."

"What?" He straightened in his seat. "You hate it here. Why would you move back?"

"Well, I haven't decided if I'll move yet, but I miss the place. I never thought I'd say those words, but there you have it. I miss home. It's been... hard. I suppose that's how I'd put it. The past couple of years have been difficult. I'm ready to settle, to put down roots, and this is where I should do that."

Franklin's lips pursed. "That doesn't sound particularly convincing."

Nicole reached across the table between them, pushing aside a bowl of beef and black bean, to take his hand. Her touch took him by surprise, familiar and yet strange all at the same time.

"Frankie, I know I hurt you and I'll always regret that."

He nodded. "Okay."

"I'm sorry."

Her words prompted a tightening in his chest. "Thank you. That means a lot to me."

"I was so young, I didn't understand what we had was special. I've spent the past five years looking for someone as kind, strong, and good as you, and I've come up empty-handed. You're the one who got away." Her eyes glistened. "I know this is a lot for you to take in, but I've been thinking about it for a while. I think we should give it another try."

"You want to get back together?" He pulled his hand away from hers.

Her face fell. She blinked.

"Yes, I want to stay with you. I think we're good together, and I know you haven't moved on."

"How do you know that?" he asked.

She offered a wobbly smile. "I stay in touch with people in town."

"Steph?" he asked.

She shook her head. "No, not Steph. She hasn't spoken to me since I left. She was angry on your behalf."

He nodded. "Well, you're right — I'm not seeing anyone. But that doesn't mean we should start things up again. You left for a reason, Nic. You weren't happy. I didn't realise you felt the way you did, but it doesn't change the fact that you couldn't be faithful to me, you couldn't stay and work things out. You wanted to move on, see other people, and even if you can't remember the reasons for that now — those reasons were real enough for you to treat me the way you did. I don't see how any of that has changed."

She pushed curls away from her face with both hands, her lower lip trembling. "But it has changed — because I've changed. I realised I was wrong, that we were good together. I was too young to see it at the time, I thought I needed to go out into the world to find my place. But it turns out, my place might well be here after all. I don't know for certain where I fit, but I do know I haven't found myself out there." She waved a hand in the direction of the dark windows that lined one wall of the restaurant.

He sighed. She was lost, that much was clear. But he wasn't convinced the Cove was the place where she'd find that sense of home she was looking for. She'd wanted nothing more than to leave the town, and him, behind five years earlier. How much could things change in that short amount of time?

"I don't know, Nic."

"You need time."

"Maybe, but the thing is — I'm not sure I could ever trust you again. How could I know whether you'll feel the same way tomorrow as you do today?"

She shrugged, shook her head. "I suppose you'll have to trust me."

"See, that's the hard part for me." He took a sip of water, then pushed his plate back. His appetite was gone. "I'll always have a place in my heart for you — we were best friends for so long, then we fell in love, and I thought we'd spend the rest of our lives together. But I don't think I can go to that place again, where I give you my whole heart. Because you tore it out the last time and it hasn't fully recovered."

CHAPTER 13

BEN

*A*fter spending some time with his parents in Brisbane he landed a programming job, for which it turned out he could do most of his work from home. All he had to do was show up at the office about once a week. He was disappointed he hadn't been able to find a position in another field of work, but since he didn't know what he wanted to do yet, he'd decided to stick with programming until he could figure it out.

He timed the drive to Emerald Cove and found it was a comfortable ninety-minute commute from Brisbane, so he found a house to rent in the beach community just one street away from the water. It was a single-story brick home, squat and cosy, without much light inside. Much like other homes in the area, it'd been built in the 1980s.

Ben pushed a box of books into one corner of the room he'd designated as his office and straightened and pressed both hands to the small of his back with a grimace. He wasn't as young as he used to be and had spent the entire day moving boxes into the new house. A dull ache in his back plus a tender knee were the result of all his efforts. The movers had loaded his furniture in the day before, and today it was beginning to feel like home.

The whooshing of waves crashing to shore was a constant backdrop to his work, something he was going to have to get used to. There weren't any waves in Townsville since the entire shoreline was protected by the Great Barrier Reef. The beaches there had been more like mud flats and held little interest for him. He was excited to spend time swimming in the ocean, walking along the sand, and otherwise loving the fact that it was a short, five-minute walk to the beach from his new home.

He moved to the office window, peered out, and combed fingers through his hair as a gentle breeze cooled the sweat that soaked his entire body from tip to toe. With a sigh of relief, he let his eyes drift shut. It was hot in the Cove, thought not as hot as it'd been up north.

As much as he'd been afraid to make such a significant change in his life, he was already feeling happier and more settled since the move down south a few days earlier. He'd been stuck in a rut for so long, it was time he did something to shake things up a bit. Besides that, he was looking forward to getting to know his biological family better, although even the thought of it had nerves jangling in his gut.

Ben arranged some of the paperwork on his desk, opened his laptop and logged on. He stood where the chair should be, eying the room in search of it. Never mind, his office chair must be somewhere in the house or garage; he'd find it later. He pulled a box over to the desk and sat on it instead, finding himself a little shorter than he'd normally be as the computer screen blinked to life.

There were emails from work, ready for him to get started on Monday. He scanned them quickly, seeing a few from the HR department asking for paperwork to be completed, and made a mental note to do it later. There was one from Mum, lamenting the fact that he'd moved to the Cove when he could've stayed with them in Brisbane and visited Diana and Andrew whenever he felt the need. A rock of guilt formed in his stomach as he read. He'd lived up north for long enough that lately his parents had let him know — in their subtle ways — that they'd always hoped their only child would move closer to them now they'd passed the eighty-year mark.

Maybe he'd do it one day. For now, this was something he had to do. He'd let Diana and Andy know he would be in the Cove for a while, that he'd rented this house and hoped to catch up with them both. Already he'd noticed a difference between his biological parents — Diana had called him back immediately to ask him all about the move and expressed her delight at seeing him again soon; Andy hadn't responded yet.

Finished scrolling through his emails, Ben reached for his phone and texted Diana and Andy again. Would they meet him for coffee that afternoon at the Emerald Cove Cafe? He was in town and would love to see them. If he didn't hear back from them both within the hour, he'd give them a call. The last time he'd seen his biological father, Andy had given the impression he would be keen to spend time together, but, so far, his attempts to reach out hadn't yielded a result — he hoped there was a simple explanation, and he supposed he'd find out soon enough.

Grateful that the internet connection he'd set up seemed to be functioning, he got to work organising his office the way he liked it. Ergonomic keyboard and mouse, two oversized monitors attached to a slimline laptop, and a reading lamp. He found the rolling office chair in the garage and set it on top of a mat in front of the oversize timber desk.

A few of his graduation certificates and awards soon hung on the wall beside his desk, and he slumped into his chair with a sigh, linking both hands behind his head to spin slowly in his chair, admiring his handiwork.

As long as the office was set up ready to begin the new job, everything else could wait. He'd eat takeaway if he had to, so the kitchen wasn't a priority. It was the way his life had always been — work came first, everything else second.

Lately, though, he'd lost enthusiasm for his line of work. Perhaps having a new place of employment would bring the spark back, although working from home it wasn't likely to feel much different to how it'd been working from home in Townsville.

As much as he enjoyed the flexibility, working in an office was something he missed — having the interactions with the team, the back and forth over a problem, the chatter in the kitchen, going out to lunch in the city together.

When he'd chosen to work remotely, he'd never imagined it would be for so long or that he'd miss the social aspects of office life so much. With a frustrated shake of the head, he stood slowly and stretched his arms high, one by one, easing the tension from his muscles. What he really needed was a career change. This one had run its course. But for now, it'd have to do.

* * *

AN IBIS DUG in a nearby rubbish bin as Ben strode into the cafe, its white head bobbing for anything tasty. Wings flapped as Ben passed, and it sailed back to the footpath, a chip in its long, curved beak.

Ben checked his watch; he was five minutes early to meet Diana and Andy. He'd been surprised to find text messages confirming the coffee date after he'd hung the few framed photographs he owned in the hallway. He chose to take it as a sign that his biological parents intended to put in the effort to get to know him, although that didn't prevent the jitters in his stomach as the waitress showed him to an empty table for three.

He sat, one foot tapping out a rhythm on the tiled floor while he waited. A plane buzzed by overhead as shoppers wearing denim shorts, colourful singlet tops or long, strapless dresses, hurried past in clusters, their arms laden with bags from the various boutiques that dotted the thoroughfare.

Diana arrived and was shown to their table. He stood to kiss her cheek then sat across from her. She smiled, her cheeks pink as she met his gaze.

"It's so good to see you again. I still can't quite believe you've moved to the Cove."

He shrugged. "I can't believe it either, but here I am."

She squeezed his hand. "Will it just be the two of us today?"

"I've invited Andy as well."

"Oh."

"That's okay, isn't it? I hope I haven't put my foot in it."

She pushed a smile onto her face. "No, of course it's fine. Things between us are a little tense because... well, never mind that."

"No, you can tell me. I mean, if you want to."

Her lips pursed. "I don't know if I should."

"All right."

"I might as well, you'll hear it from someone else if I don't say anything."

"Okay." He braced himself. There wasn't much he knew about his biological father, other than the fact that Andy and Diana had been teenagers when he was born and hadn't stayed together. Also, that Andy hadn't known about his existence until a few weeks earlier.

"As you may know, Andy was married to my best friend — Cindy. Do you remember Cindy?"

"Yes, of course," he replied with a smile. "She lives next to Seaside Manor, your inn."

"My former inn."

"Right."

"Well, they broke up fairly recently because he had an affair with a younger woman."

"Oh." It hurt to think his father might treat Cindy that way, although he couldn't judge since he knew nothing of their situation.

"Anyway, he and his girlfriend have recently moved back to the Cove, so it's a little tense. Also, Cindy didn't know about you, or that Andy and I had our...

fling I suppose you'd call it... back when we were teenagers. She and Andy were already dating at the time, so it came as a bit of a shock to her when you showed up last month. We're fine now, but there was some tension between us."

His brow furrowed. "Oh, I'm sorry to hear that. I didn't realise..."

"Of course you didn't. I hated to say anything to you about it because it's not something you should have to worry yourself over. Only, now that you're living here, I'm sure you'll find out and I'd rather it came from me." She rearranged the salt and pepper shakers on the table, her hands trembling.

"I'm sorry," he said.

She shook her head, squeezed his hand again. "None of that. Nothing for you to be sorry about. Anyway, it's all behind us now. I'm so glad Andy is meeting us here; it's only right you can get to know each other."

The fact that Diana hadn't told Andy about his birth and adoption all those years ago still weighed heavy on Ben's mind. When he'd discovered that during his first visit to see her, he'd been shocked but had accepted it without question. Now that he'd had time to mull it over, it ate at him a little bit more every day. Would things have been different if Andy had known? Maybe he would've stood up to Diana's parents, demanded they give him a chance to raise his son. It was something he'd always wonder about, but never know for certain.

Ten minutes later, Andy finally arrived. He rushed in, his greying, blondish hair askew as he hurried to the table. His grin was wide and infectious as he shook Ben's hand and sat.

"Sorry I'm late. I hope I haven't missed anything important. Hello Di. Good to see you again, Ben."

"You too," replied Ben, marvelling again as he had done the last time over how charismatic his biological father was. No one had ever accused Ben of having charisma; he was more the quiet, studious type. He certainly hadn't inherited that trait from his father, although they shared the same strong, straight nose. Perhaps there was more they had in common, things they could bond over.

It all felt a little strange — he had a father, one who'd raised him and who'd taken him camping, fishing, four-wheel driving, and swimming countless times. They'd enjoyed the same things, spent time together laughing and talking, or sitting in silence with rods hung over the water, lines dangling as they waited for fish to bite. He'd never wanted for anything throughout his childhood — except this: to get to know his biological parents and find out if they had some kind of connection. He'd often wondered why they'd given him up. Now he had a kind of answer for that. Still, he longed to discover more about them.

They chatted about the weather, Ben's new house, what it was like to live in the Cove. As time passed, Ben noticed the tension between Diana and Andy dissolve like honey stirred into a cup of hot tea.

"So, ever been married?" asked Andy, out of the blue.

Ben shook his head. "No."

Andy's brows arched. "Really? A handsome fella like you?"

Ben shrugged. "I came close once, but it didn't work out."

Andy and Diana exchanged a look. Ben recognised

the look — they were plotting. He wished they wouldn't. His adoptive parents had set him up enough times over the years for him to know it wouldn't change anything. He wasn't looking for love, contrary to what most people expected of him.

He was perfectly content living on his own. He hadn't been in his thirties, but now in his forties he'd accepted that this is how his life would be. He liked his own company, had plenty of hobbies to keep himself busy. The only thing that bothered him sometimes was the loneliness, and perhaps he could do something about that by joining the surf club or volunteering at an animal shelter on the Gold Coast — he'd done plenty of volunteering over the years and it always boosted his spirits.

Diana patted the back of his hand. "Don't worry, honey, there are plenty of lovely, single gals in the Cove."

"Really, I'm fine. I'm not looking for a relationship."

Andy huffed. "I don't know how you do that. I've never been any good at being alone, but good on you, Ben. You're a strong man — don't see much of myself in you and that's a good thing I think."

Ben's brow furrowed. "I don't know about that."

Andy clapped him on the shoulder. "You're a better man than I am, I can tell that already." His eyes glistened. "I hope you'll take some time to get to know your brother, Ethan. The two of you would really hit it off, I think."

Ben dipped his head in agreement. "I'm looking forward to it."

CHAPTER 14

REBECCA

*T*he hum of telephones and conversation lifted Rebecca's spirits as she pored over the stack of paperwork on her desk. There was nothing worse than red tape and forms in her opinion; she'd much rather be outside with the sun on her face, walking around the Cove. She loved getting in amongst the community. She'd been there long enough now that most of the locals recognised her and offered her a smile or a wave. She only had to get through the rest of this stack, and she could be out the door.

With a sigh, she reached for another form and pulled it across the desk, pen poised. Since her time off, Franklin had tasked her with most of the station's paperwork. She wasn't sure why he was punishing her for something completely out of her control. Or perhaps he was concerned she'd get hurt again. The sad fact was, in her short time on the job she'd already been rushed to hospital with injuries twice. Hardly a stellar record. If she wanted him to ease up on the desk patrol, she'd have to make sure not to get injured again to prove to him she wasn't a magnet for it.

She watched as the rest of the team filed into the board room for a meeting about a sting operation they were coordinating with the water police. She wasn't involved —Franklin had made a point of telling her that earlier in the day. They needed her to stay in town to make sure everything was under control while they ran the operation.

With a shake of her head, she returned her attention to the mind-numbing work on her desk.

"Officer needed in reception immediately." Steph's calm voice called over the sound system.

Rebecca leapt to her feet and jogged across the office. The door swung shut behind her as she hurried into the reception area. A woman stood in the middle of the room, a baby in her arms. The woman swayed and spun, her eyes wide, movements frantic.

"What's wrong?" asked Rebecca as she drew close.

The woman shook her head. "I don't know, I think she's choking." Her voice keened at a high pitch, her eyes red-rimmed.

"Let me see her."

Rebecca took the baby, as the mother shifted from foot to foot, wringing her hands and sobbing quietly. Steph appeared at Rebecca's side as she ran through the health checks she'd practiced so many times before.

"Thanks, Constable. I don't think the baby's breathing. I've called the ambulance, but they're ten minutes out."

"Not to worry," said Rebecca in a reassuring voice, even as her heart thundered against her ribcage.

"She's choking on something," sobbed the woman. "I think it's a piece of carrot. I didn't give it to her, but she must've grabbed it from my bowl of salad when I looked away because she was clutching a piece of it in her hand when I noticed she couldn't breathe. Please help her."

She checked the baby's mouth for an obstruction, then turned it over and tapped it hard on the back. Two more taps and the baby sucked in a deep breath and began to wail. The woman grabbed the baby with a shout of relief, held the child to her chest in a bear hug as tears streamed down her cheeks.

Rebecca took a step back, adrenaline cooling in her veins. Steph slapped her gently on the shoulder. "Great work, Constable."

She nodded in response, smiling in relief. Just then, Franklin strode through the door, a frown creasing his forehead. Steph explained what'd happened while Rebecca talked to the grateful mother who rocked the baby against her chest, silent tears still streaking her cheeks.

When the paramedics arrived, Rebecca waved goodbye and headed back into the office. As the door shut behind her, she found Franklin had followed her inside.

"From what Steph told me, you did great work, Proby."

"Thanks, boss. Just doing my job."

"Well, any day you save a life is a good day on the job."

She nodded. "That's the truth. I was feeling a bit

down about all the paperwork, but this reminded me why I love being a police officer."

He fell into step beside her. "I know I've been giving you a hard time but you need to go steady getting back into things. You've had a rough few months, so it doesn't hurt you to get some peace and quiet."

She shrugged. "I know."

"You'll have plenty of opportunities to get out and about, don't worry about that. Are you well, other than the paperwork?"

His brown eyes found hers, sending a jolt of electricity through her body that took her by surprise. She ran a hand over her smooth ponytail. "I'm fine. Thanks for asking. How about you? I see you've met someone."

His eyebrows shot skyward. "Huh?"

"The blonde," she replied, wondering at his seeming lack of understanding. "The one you brought into the office."

"Oh, Nicole you mean?"

She nodded. "Yeah, don't tell me you've already forgotten her. It wasn't that long ago."

His cheeks reddened. "We're not dating."

"Really? It sure looked as though she was comfortable around you."

"We used to be engaged. It's a long story for another day, but let's just say she's in town and we're spending some time hanging out."

"Oh. So, you're not getting back together?"

His lips pursed. "I'm not sure I can really define what's going on right now between us."

Her heart fell. "I see. Well, I think you should give it a chance. If she makes you happy, you should see where things might go."

His eyes narrowed. "Really?"

"Yeah, why not?"

He pressed his hands to his hips, stared off into the distance for a moment. "I suppose there's no reason I shouldn't. Well, see you around, Proby."

He strode away, leaving Rebecca staring after him, her throat tight with emotion. She'd given him an opening, a chance to tell her he wasn't looking for a relationship with his ex-fiancée, that he had feelings for someone else. But he hadn't done that — hadn't hesitated or even looked her way as he spoke. She didn't know he'd been engaged before. That seemed like something Steph might've shared with her, even if Franklin was unwilling.

With a sigh, she returned to her desk, slouched in the chair, and reached for another form to complete.

* * *

FRANKLIN

The office seemed smaller than usual. Franklin tapped at his keyboard, his mind elsewhere. He re-read an email he was writing, realised it didn't make sense, grunted in frustration, and linked his hands behind his head.

Bec had basically pushed him into giving Nicole another chance. He couldn't understand why she'd do that. Or why her words bothered him so much. So what if she didn't care who he was dating, that shouldn't matter to him. He was her boss, nothing more than that. Still, she didn't have to be quite so unconcerned about the idea of him getting back together with his ex-fiancée.

It was all such a confusing mess.

He didn't like it when things got overly emotional or complicated. Right now, he couldn't seem to get a handle on how he felt about anything. It'd been nice to see Nicole after so many years, but at the same time he didn't feel that tug of romantic love he'd felt for her in the past. He loved her, but it was more of a familiar, friendly kind of love.

He shook his head and decided to get a coffee. Maybe, when he returned to his desk, he could finish writing that email, then jump in the cruiser and patrol the Cove.

It was always good to get outside and feel the sun on his face, taste the salt in the air. There was nothing better than spending time outdoors in the Cove at this time of year. Summer was just around the corner, but the oppressive heat hadn't yet settled over the town. It was warm enough to swim or surf, but the breeze was pleasant, and the azure water sparkled even as humpback whales sailed through the Cove, breaching and spouting as they made their way south.

"Hey, boss," said Steph.

She was in the kitchen making a coffee with one of those little pods that he had so much trouble with. He preferred instant, since the pods always seemed to get stuck in the machine, or open too soon, or fall on the floor right as he stepped forward. He disliked complicated coffee almost as much as he hated complicated emotions.

"How's it going today?" he asked. "The twins giving you trouble?"

She rolled her eyes. "Always. They're starting kindergarten next year if you can believe it."

He shook his head. "Wow, that went fast."

"Tell me about it. I've been so sleep deprived, running on empty, feeling like I can't manage it all and that it'll be that way forever. And just like that, they'll be going to kindy three days a week. Next thing I know they'll be in school."

"Feel like upping your hours here then?" he asked with a chuckle. "We can always make your life busier, if that's how you like it."

"No thank you, working mornings at the station suits me perfectly. And now I'll have a couple of afternoons a week to myself to do whatever I want."

"You could lay around the house, get your nails done, or whatever it is women do when they have spare time," offered Franklin, stirring sugar into his coffee.

She huffed. "You don't have a clue about women, do you, boss?"

He shrugged. "Mum died when I was a tyke, so I've never actually lived with a woman, but I'm guessing you like to be pampered. It's in all the ads on TV anyway."

She laughed. "Come on now, I know you dated Nicole for years. You must've learned a few things about women."

Franklin loved to tease Steph. The way her cheeks reddened, her laughter. It was too much fun not to try to get her going just a little bit. Still, there was some truth to his words — women confounded him at times. He'd thought he knew Bec pretty well, thought maybe she even had feelings for him other than as a boss. But he'd been wrong about that, as he'd been almost every other time he'd tried to figure out what the woman in his life was thinking.

When Nicole left him, he hadn't seen it coming,

had thought whatever problems they had could be worked through — they loved each other, surely that meant they'd figure it out. But that wasn't what'd happened.

She'd cheated on him — not once, he'd discovered afterwards, but with several different men who lived in the Cove. Men he knew, some he thought of as friends. No one had thought to tell him what was going on, except his best friend and partner at the time, who'd shared what he'd heard. Franklin hadn't listened to him, had shouted at him that he didn't know what he was talking about, since Nicole wouldn't do such a thing — and he'd been wrong. About her, about all of it. So, what made him think he'd be any better now at understanding what Nicole wanted, or how Bec felt?

"Maybe you're right," he replied.

Steph nodded, a smile brightening her face. "There's hope for you yet, boss."

He laughed. "Don't go that far."

"I have a feeling."

Franklin poured milk into his cup and set the carton back in the fridge. "Maybe you're right."

He carried a steaming hot cup of coffee back to his desk, sat, pushed his shoulders back, and reached for the mouse. His mobile rang and he pulled it from his pocket and pressed it to his ear as he set about re-typing the email.

The voice on the other end of the phone was familiar. It was one of the nurses from his father's nursing home. His hands fell away from the keyboard and he straightened in his seat.

"Is he okay?"

"He's had another stroke. The ambulance left five minutes ago, he's on his way to the hospital."

When Franklin hung up the phone, dread settled like a rock in his gut. His throat tightened and he coughed to dislodge the lump forming there. No time to get upset, he had to hurry to the hospital to be there for his father. But another stroke, whew. He'd seen how much devastation the last one had wrought on his father's health. Surely, he couldn't survive something like that again. But if anyone could, it'd be his father — he'd been tough his whole life: fit, strong, resilient. There was a chance he'd make it through, Franklin had to believe that.

He grabbed his car keys and headed for the door. No need to tell anyone else what was going on yet. Better to find out more before saying anything. He dipped a head in Bec's direction before hurrying past Steph who called something out at his retreating back. He'd talk to her later. Right now, he couldn't think about anything but getting to the hospital to be by his father's side.

CHAPTER 15

REBECCA

*F*eet pounded the hard sand as Rebecca ducked under the branches of a squat bush that crowded the winding trail. The sound of waves punctuated the still, cool air, receding as she ran.

Sweat trickled down the sides of her face. Her strength was returning, her fitness increasing with each workout, each time she pushed herself. Her hand still hurt if she bumped it accidentally, but that too was improving. It wouldn't be long before the entire incident with her ex was behind her and she could move forward with her life and forget all about him.

Well, maybe she wouldn't forget. But she could let it go. Let him go. Let go the part of her that'd been hiding from him, scared for so long. She wasn't scared anymore.

The thought buoyed her sagging spirits.

Most of the time she felt good and was happy to embrace her new life with her real name, a good job, friends and even visits from family. But today was one of those days when she wasn't sure what she was fighting for anymore, it was all so overwhelming.

Mum had returned to Sydney. Franklin wasn't at the office when she'd left for the day to meet her mother and drive her to the airport. She didn't know where he'd disappeared to; he hadn't said a word when he left the office. If he was out on a case, he could've taken her with him. But even Steph didn't seem to know what was going on. Which led Rebecca to believe he'd gone to meet Nicole.

Not that it should matter to her, although it was highly unprofessional of him not to communicate to Steph about where he'd be since he was on duty.

She shook her head, brow furrowed.

What was going on with her? This was the life she'd wanted, had fought for, longed for. Now it was here, and all she could do was complain. She should be grateful, happy even. That's why she'd decided to go for a run — hoping it would clear her thoughts, give her a boost of much-needed serotonin. Or something like that, anyway. So far, all she had to show for it was a stitch in one side and some kind of scratch on her calf muscle from a plant or shrub that she didn't remember stumbling across.

The winding, sandy path soon entered a quaint neighbourhood. It ended in a clumsy fade of sand into grass, where Rebecca stepped over the curb and onto the bitumen. She slowed to a walk, pressed both hands to her hips, and studied her surroundings, squinting against the harsh afternoon sunlight. Where was she?

She'd traveled almost every street in the Cove multiple times since moving there, usually in the cruiser. But she hadn't run this trail before and wasn't sure which neighbourhood it had brought her to.

Tenting a hand over her eyes, she puffed hard, her laboured breathing slowly returning to normal as she scanned the street. She knew this street. Steph lived here, somewhere. Breaking into a steady jog, she made her way past single-story suburban brick homes with faded lawns, discarded bicycles, and clumps of greenery in curved garden beds.

There it was. Steph's house was one of the few with two stories — in a brownish brick, it stood out from the rest of the street due to the white trim around the windows and roof. Steph's garden was just as faded as the rest since they'd barely had rain in months. And with water restrictions in place, no one could water their lawns or gardens without a full rainwater tank in the back yard.

Thoughts of Franklin swirled at the edge of her mind as she ambled closer to the house. It wasn't right for him to take off halfway through the day and not tell anyone where he was going. What if there'd been an emergency? It would've taken time to find him; if he'd been out of reach, they would have had to call in the night crew, meanwhile she would've had to manage things on her own. The rest of the team had left early as well, each with their own caseload to manage. By mid-afternoon, she had been the only one left at the station since Steph spent afternoons with her twins.

The more she thought about it, the more riled she became. Her already warm cheeks flamed hotter, her heartbeat sped up, and her nostrils flared. She could've called him, but that wasn't the point.

She had to get it off her chest, and who better to talk to about it all than Steph.

The doorbell chimed, and a large dog launched itself at the other side of the door. Rebecca stumbled back a few steps, her pulse racing. When the door opened, Steph offered her a smile even as she stood hunched, holding onto the collar of a large, German Shepherd doing its best impression of a rabid beast.

"Don't worry, he's friendly. Come on in," puffed Steph, heaving at the dog's collar.

Rebecca arched an eyebrow, took a tentative step forward. "Yeah, he looks it."

She brushed past the dog and into a wide, open living room. Twin boys tore around the living room on small plastic trikes, chasing each other across the white tiled floor and shouting at the top of their lungs.

"Let's go outside," said Steph, her voice raised as she pointed at the glass sliding door that led out to a backyard.

With a nod, Rebecca followed her. Steph let the dog loose in the yard, then turned to face Rebecca with a sigh. Rebecca was grateful the dog completely ignored her, more interested in chasing off a Willy Wagtail dipping its tail as if to taunt the dog from the side of an enormous black trampoline.

"It's so nice to see you outside of work," said Steph, kissing her cheek and motioning to a pair of plastic chairs.

She sank into one and Rebecca sat beside her.

"I was running along the beach and got a bit lost. Found myself on your street," she said.

Steph laughed. "Wow, you really ran a long way,

huh? We're right on the edge of town. Nowhere near your unit."

"I guess so." Rebecca leaned forward, resting her arms on her thighs as she watched the dog sniff its way across the large, open backyard.

"What's up?" asked Steph.

"You know how you said Franklin left without telling you where he went?"

Steph dipped her head.

"It's still bothering me. I mean, why would he do that? It isn't like him to do something like that. If there's one thing I've learned about the boss, it's that he's very, very responsible. I mean, to a fault."

Steph's lips pursed. "You're right about that."

"So, what's going on? Has he called you? Is he losing focus on the job now that this Nicole's back in his life? Did he go out to meet her and just forget that the rest of us need him?" Irritation boiled in her chest the longer she talked. It really was selfish of him to act that way, not to consider their needs — her needs. She still needed him — she was inexperienced, injured — what could she do without him there to help her if something went wrong?

Steph sighed deeply, pulling Rebecca back into the moment. She pressed both hands to her face, her eyes darkening.

"What? What is it?" Rebecca straightened in her seat, dread pooling in her gut.

"It's nothing to do with Nicole. It's his dad. He didn't want me to say anything to anyone about it just yet, but he's in the hospital again. He called me about an hour ago."

Rebecca's heart fell. Guilt thickened in her throat. "Oh, wow. That's terrible."

"I know, he's pretty upset."

"I feel so bad. All those things I said."

"Don't worry about it," replied Steph. "You didn't know. It must've seemed strange to you that he left without saying anything, I'm sure. I've been worried about him ever since I got home, so didn't have a chance to think about how you were taking it all. I'm sorry I couldn't tell you more."

"It's okay. I can't believe I was such a jerk — all day I've been so angry with him."

"You're not a jerk."

Rebecca shook her head, stood, and paced across the concrete patio, then back again. "What happened? Do you know more than that?"

Steph shook her head. "I don't know. He didn't say, and he had that tone in his voice."

"The 'don't ask' tone?" asked Rebecca, chewing her lower lip.

"That's the one."

Rebecca's mobile phone buzzed in the zipped pocket on her leggings. She unzipped the pocket, pulled out her phone. Franklin's name lit up the screen.

"Hello?"

"Hey, Proby." His tired voice, thick with emotion, brought more guilt crashing in.

"Where are you?" she asked.

He hesitated. "Dad's in the hospital. He had another stroke. They're working on him now, I'm in the waiting room." His voice trailed away.

"Is Nicole there with you?" she asked. No matter how she felt about the situation, he needed someone by his side at the hospital. Someone to be there for him, to help him through whatever happened next.

He grunted. "Uh, no."

"Where is she?"

"I don't know. Why do you ask, Proby? She's not exactly on my mind right now, I've got other things going on." The usual irritation laced his voice, bringing a smile to her face even as her eyes glistened with unshed tears for his father.

"I'm coming to the hospital," she said before she'd even had a chance to think about it.

Steph's eyes widened.

"You don't have to do that," his objection was half-hearted, weak, as if he didn't mean it.

"Yes, I'm coming. I'll see you there in about half an hour, okay?"

He sighed. "Thanks, Proby."

She hung up the phone, pushed it back into her pocket and pressed both hands to her forehead, her mind racing.

"So?" pressed Steph.

"Another stroke," replied Rebecca, willing herself not to cry. She hadn't known Franklin's father for long, but she'd grown to care about him — he reminded her a lot of Franklin, or perhaps it was the other way around. Either way, she knew how much Franklin loved his dad, and it was that understanding that caused the lump to grow in her throat.

"So, you're going to the hospital?"

Rebecca nodded. "But I've got to get home first. I'll grab my wallet and car, since I'll probably have to buy him dinner. I'm sure he's not thinking about eating but just in case."

"He'd probably appreciate that."

"And I should really shower before I go."

Steph's nose wrinkled. "I think that would be wise."

* * *

THE HOSPITAL WAS QUIET, only one other family in the emergency waiting room when Rebecca arrived. Franklin sat on one of the plastic chairs, his head in his hands, hair disheveled.

"Hey, boss."

She sat beside him and he startled at the sound of her voice, glanced sideways at her. "Proby, you shouldn't sneak up on people that way."

"Sorry, I'll make sure to announce myself next time."

He grunted in response. "Thanks for coming."

"Do you need anything? A coffee, something to eat?"

He straightened, shook his head. "No thanks. I'm waiting to hear what's going on. I haven't had an update in half an hour, I'm starting to get worried. Why won't they let me see him?"

She sighed. "I'm sorry, that must be really hard. Do you know anything about what they're doing?"

"They gave him some kind of medication to restore blood flow when he first arrived. When I got here, he was getting an MRI or something, so I couldn't see him. Now, I have no idea what's happening." Frustration edged his voice, and he rubbed his eyes with his fingertips.

They sat in silence for a few minutes. Rebecca watched the hands on a clock hung on the opposite wall as the seconds ticked by.

"What am I going to do without him?" asked Franklin, his voice low.

Rebecca rested a hand on his shoulder, her heart

aching for him. "Don't talk like that. We don't know anything yet."

"I know, but it's only a matter of time. He's my family, I don't have anyone else — no one I'm close to, anyway. I have cousins, but they live hours away and I hardly ever see them or talk to them. It's been me and Dad for most of my life. I don't know how to face it all without him." His voice broke, he covered his face with both hands. When his hands fell away, his usual stoic expression had returned.

The fact that Franklin had lost his partner and best friend, along with a broken engagement, in the years before Rebecca moved to the Cove no doubt added to his loneliness. With Nicole back in the area, perhaps she was just what he needed. Although when she'd asked him earlier if Nicole was there, he'd seemed surprised at the question.

"You're not alone, Franklin." She hardly ever used his name when she spoke to him. "You have an entire community of people who care about you. And you've got Nicole as well."

He gave her side-eye. "Yeah, I guess so. But sometimes I feel completely alone without Dad." He sighed and stared down at his hands, palms up as they rested in his lap.

Rebecca reached over, laced her fingers through his and squeezed his hand. "You're not alone. I'm here."

When he met her gaze, emotion pooled in her gut. The depth of sadness in his eyes made her want to throw her arms around him and hold him close. She resisted the urge — what he needed now was her friendship. If she crossed the line, he'd push her away, then he would be here alone, and she couldn't do that to him.

"Thanks, Bec. I really appreciate you being here. Let's get that drink. The coffee here is like tar, but the tea isn't bad."

She released his hand as they walked together towards the cafeteria. "Sounds good to me."

CHAPTER 16

CINDY

*T*he tray of glasses wobbled on her hand. Cindy bit down on her lower lip as she carried it from the kitchen. Mineral water, lemonade, lemon lime and bitters — six tall glasses in all, filled with ice and soda, and all teetering as her arm struggled to hold them high.

She reached the kitchen door and turned to push her way through it, instead it slapped her in the rear as Crystal rushed into the kitchen carrying a pile of dirty dishes.

The tray tipped one way, then the other, falling with a crash to the floor as Cindy yelped in dismay.

"Whoops, sorry," said Crystal.

"It's not your fault," replied Cindy with a shake of her head. "I shouldn't carry so many glasses. It's just that we're ultra-busy today and I didn't want to have to make two trips."

"I can clean it up," offered Crystal.

"No, I'll do it. Can you please redo the drinks order for table five?"

When she'd first hired Crystal, newly arrived in Australia from Bangkok, the girl hardly knew how to hold a mop, let alone wait tables. Over the three years since, Crystal had studied in a local university, and worked part-time in the Emerald Cafe, and had become an invaluable member of the team there. Cindy couldn't imagine what she'd do without her these days. Besides that, she'd discovered early on that Crystal had the voice of an angel, and had given her a regular weekend gig playing live music at the cafe — which always drew a good crowd.

With a nod, Crystal set off to fill the order. Cindy headed for the storage cupboard in the back of the kitchen and found the broom, mop, and bucket. She got to work cleaning up the mess, moving as fast as she could since it was a slipping hazard and the last thing she needed now was for someone to fall in her kitchen.

As she swept glass shards into a dustpan, a feeling of utter fatigue washed over her. She'd been doing this for too long. It seemed as though every moment of her life now was dedicated to working at the cafe, especially as they drew closer to the peak summer months. What she really needed was a break. Some time off to regroup after everything that'd happened in her life in recent months.

Perhaps she should get out of town and take a holiday before the summer months.

With a sigh, she carried the dustpan to the bin and tipped the broken glass into it. Then, she set about filling the mop bucket with hot, sudsy water.

The idea of taking a holiday somewhere alone made her throat tighten and her eyes water. She drew the mop from the bucket, hot water dripping.

A holiday on her own.

After so many years traveling with a husband and her three children, she couldn't imagine going somewhere alone. Maybe it wouldn't be so bad. Still, what would she do with her time? Where should she go? She imagined herself sunbathing beside a beautiful pool with crystal clear water in an oversized hat and dark sunglasses, with a book in one hand — surrounded by strangers. She shook her head, scrubbing harder than was strictly necessary with the mop across the tiled floor.

She and Athol had been dating for a while, but she wasn't the kind of woman to go on a holiday with a man who wasn't her husband — young people these days did it often enough, she knew that, but it wasn't how things were done when she was a girl. She'd stuck with the morals she'd been raised with so far in her life and wasn't about to shuck them now.

Crystal reappeared at her side, a pencil stuck behind one ear, her long, dark hair pulled into a messy bun.

"You okay?" she asked.

Cindy leaned on the end of the mop handle, puffing. "Yes, thank you, honey."

"What's up? You've gone all red and blotchy," said Crystal, waving a hand at Cindy.

She glanced down to find that her neck was indeed covered in reddish patches, the way it often did when she felt emotional or anxious.

"I was thinking about taking some time off — having a holiday."

Crystal grinned, her dark eyes sparkling. "I think it's a great idea. You need a break; you work too hard."

"I know, only I'd have to go alone and I'm not sure I'm up for that."

"Why alone?" Crystal's nose wrinkled. "You could go with one of your kids."

It wasn't a bad idea. "Maybe, but Sarah is so busy with her new husband and writing her book, and Ethan has the bed and breakfast to run. I don't know."

"What about Adele?" Crystal chewed on a fingernail.

Cindy shrugged. "I suppose she might do it. She's been a bit stressed lately, though. Maybe I should visit her — I've heard Darwin is a lovely place to visit and I've never been there."

"Sounds like a plan," replied Crystal.

She hurried off while Cindy emptied the mop water into the sink. She put everything away and headed for her office, dropping into the rolling chair with a grunt. It felt good to sit, to get off her aching feet for a few minutes.

Crystal could manage on her own for a while, since the lunch rush was almost over.

She dialled Adele's number, put it on speaker, and leaned back in her chair.

"Hello?"

"Hey, love, how are you?"

"I'm okay, I guess." The sadness in her daughter's voice broke Cindy's heart. Adele had always been a happy child; that was something Cindy had never had to worry about.

"I thought I might come for a visit. Would that be okay?"

Adele's voice rose a notch. "Come here? Really? That would be great, Mum."

"Perfect, it's settled then. I'm flying to Darwin."

"How long can you stay?"

"Maybe a week. The cafe will get busier for the summer before much longer. This would be the perfect time to get away."

After she hung up the phone, Cindy couldn't stop smiling. She could take a break from work and her life in the Cove, while visiting her daughter at the same time. Adele had told her she had a few days off work the next week due to her shift schedule, so the two of them could spend plenty of time together. It would also give them a chance to talk about what was going on in Adele's life — Cindy felt so out of the loop these days when it came to her youngest child.

CINDY SHUT the office door behind her, smiling as she left for the day. She was leaving early, something she rarely did, but now that she had a plan all she wanted to do was get home and pack her bags for Darwin.

The cafe was almost empty, only a few tables occupied. The sun warmed the western sky, shadows lengthening from the line of casuarina trees that dotted the fence line separating the grassy bank from the sand dunes across the street.

Cindy pushed her sunglasses into place, waved goodbye to Crystal, and headed out the door.

"Cindy!"

Someone in the cafe called her name. With a sigh, she removed the sunglasses and stepped back inside. A couple sat at one of the tables, the man waved a hand over his head.

Andy and Keisha.

There was no escaping, they'd seen her, and she'd have to say hello, but all she wanted to do was get home and prepare for her trip. Still, she should try to have a relationship of some kind with Andy, he was the father of her children and she knew how important it was to them that she get along with him and his new girlfriend.

With pursed lips she headed over to greet them, clutching her purse to her side.

"Hello, Andy, what a surprise. Keisha, it's good to see you again."

Keisha inclined her head. "Cindy, how are you?"

"I'm wonderful thank you."

"We were just talking about you," said Andy. "I thought you'd be here, but Keisha was sure you wouldn't."

"Oh?" Cindy cocked her head to one side. "Why is that?"

"The service here is terrible, I assumed that meant you were gone and your staff didn't care."

Cindy bit back a retort. "I'm sorry to hear that, is there anything I can help you with."

"I need a glass of water before I can think about what I want to eat." Keisha steepled her hands.

"Of course, I'll be happy to bring you a water. Andy, anything for you?"

Andy's cheeks reddened. "You don't have to do that, Cindy. You were on your way out; I'm sure Crystal can take care of us."

"I don't mind at all."

She strode to the kitchen and filled two glasses with water.

"Is that your ex out there?" asked Crystal, peering through the small square window in the top of the kitchen door.

Cindy grunted. "Yes it is. They want water."

Crystal's eyes widened. "Wow, I thought you'd left."

"I certainly tried."

"I'll take the water out," offered Crystal.

"No, that's fine. I'll bring them water, then I'm leaving as soon as I can."

Crystal nodded, chewed on her lower lip. "You okay?"

Cindy offered a dip of the head in response, pushed through the kitchen door, and carried the full glasses to the table.

As she drew closer to them, she overheard Keisha's high-pitched voice. "I'm only saying we should eat somewhere else. The food here isn't that good anyway, and it's weird."

"We can't leave now, it'd be rude," replied Andy.

Cindy slowed her pace, ears burning.

"Why do you care?"

"I don't want to be rude."

"Fine, we can stay. But I'm not happy."

Cindy picked up the pace. "Here you go, cold water."

"Thanks," replied Andy with a warm smile.

"You're welcome." She glanced at Keisha who stared off into the distance, a sullen expression on her pretty face. "So, how's the house? Are you enjoying living back in the Cove, Keisha?"

Keisha's almond-shaped brown eyes fixed on her.

LILLY MIRREN

"The house is too dark and cold, and there's some kind smell coming from downstairs."

"There isn't a smell," interjected Andy.

"You wouldn't know, you don't have a sensitive nose like I do." She sniffed, waved a hand dismissively. "There isn't enough light in the house and I'm sure we're gonna freeze as soon as winter comes."

Andy shook his head, a smile plastered to his face. "Freeze? In Emerald Cove?"

"You know what I mean," replied Keisha with a roll of the eyes. "It's not big enough. You promised we'd have a big house."

"There's only two of us, Keisha darling."

Cindy shifted her weight from one foot to the other. As much as she relished the idea of a good roasting for her ex these days, bearing witness to it made her more than a little uncomfortable.

"Well, I'm sorry to hear that. I was on my way out, so I hope you enjoy your meals."

Andy met her gaze. "I suppose we'll see you around."

"It seems inevitable."

Cindy said her goodbyes, but as she walked away from the table she couldn't help feeling a little bit sorry for her ex. She wasn't entirely sure he'd known what he was getting himself into, although since Keisha had worked for him as his assistant for years, he really had no excuse. Perhaps in time he might even regret the way he'd treated her, his wife of almost forty years. To be fair, though, given the way everything was going, Cindy couldn't help being glad she'd been given a second chance to do things her own way in life, even if everything was so very different to how she'd always imagined it would be.

CHAPTER 17

MEG

*W*alton trotted beside Meg's feet, his black ears bobbing with each step he took. His little nose sniffed at the ground, but he didn't adjust course. He simply kept moving along, always doing what he was supposed to do. Meg smiled, at least something was going right in her life — she wasn't sure what she'd have done these last few weeks without Walton. He was her constant companion when she was at home, never judging and ever ready to snuggle on the couch.

Oscar strained at the leash Sarah held in one hand, tugging Sarah in every which direction as they power-walked through the park. Next to her, Vicky led Petal, Cindy's dog, who seemed to think she had much better things to do than walk through the park on a leash. She stopped frequently, parking her small rear end on the pavement, and refusing to budge until Vicky managed to distract her long enough with treats for them to continue on their way for a while longer.

"Should we hold your baby shower at the beach?" asked Sarah. "It'd be perfect this time of year, and we could have a BBQ in the afternoon at the park beside the beach when there's a lovely breeze. Or, were you thinking of something fancier?"

Meg shook her head. "No, that sounds perfect for us. We definitely want it to be casual, and I love the beach. But Brad wants to be involved and I don't think he'd be willing to go to the beach. I'm sorry." Tightness pulled the muscles of her neck, and a headache formed at the base of her skull.

There were so many things going on in her life at the moment it was hard for her to keep pace. She loved that her friends wanted to throw her a baby shower, but the only thing she'd been absorbed with for days now was the results of the pregnancy scan. She hadn't talked about it with anyone, not even Brad. He'd been encouraging, thoughtful, and more affectionate than usual, but otherwise hadn't raised the subject either.

Sarah bit down on her lip as Vicky piped up. "Oh, of course, we should've thought about that. He still won't go to the beach?"

"No, not yet. His entire attitude has improved so much, especially with his studies and the baby coming, but he's yet to try wheeling down to the beach. We even had the World Surfing Federation donate him a beach wheelchair so he could make it down to the water's edge. But it's still in our garage locker."

Sarah strained against Oscar as he lunged hard towards a bush that seemed particularly appealing to his outstretched, quivering nose. "Oscar! For the love of— can't you just behave like Winston?"

Meg and Vicky both chuckled at that. Meg felt the tension in her neck ease as her mood shifted. She was grateful for good friends, and walking Winston in the park always helped her feel a little better. Still, how would she manage when the baby came? She couldn't hide away from her feelings then. Couldn't duck out to the park whenever she wanted. For many years she'd told people she wouldn't ever marry or have children — she'd seen the way her parents had lived and had no desire to follow their example. Then she'd met Brad, and everything had changed — for the first time she'd longed to build a family of her own, and believed in her heart that she and Brad would do everything differently from the way she'd been raised.

But now she was scared of what motherhood might bring. The thought that her baby might have health issues consumed her during the daylight hours and at night. Her dreams had been dark and frightened, and she'd woken several times the past few nights with sweat coating her body, muscles twitching with the intense desire to run. Somewhere. Anywhere.

She'd felt this way before, when she was a teenager and the shouting matches between her parents grew violent. The need to run, to get away from the house, as far away as her legs and savings would carry her. But the dreams had settled, the irritation in her body quelled after a few months living in Emerald Cove. She'd felt peace here for the first time in her life, safety as well. But now the dreams were back, and she couldn't shake the urge to leave.

She'd never do it, of course. Her husband needed her and their baby did too. But how could she manage it all? Fear of the future overwhelmed her senses, but she pushed it back with a shake of the head. Not now. She couldn't think about it now, she'd cry or yell and neither one would do anyone any good.

Besides, she was still processing it all, and the doctor had said they couldn't be certain, that there were more tests to run. She wasn't ready to talk about it with Sarah and Vicky. She'd have to keep it bottled up a while longer. Repressing her feelings, suppressing her fears, those were things Meg was good at — she'd had plenty of practice.

With an intake of breath, she tried to focus her attention back onto the conversation. She wasn't ready to talk about the baby. Not yet.

"I mean, I get it. It's going to be hard to tackle a beach visit, I'm sure he's afraid of how it'll all work, and he misses the waves so much it's easier for him to stay away. Of course, he doesn't say any of that, I'm only guessing it's how he feels." She sighed. "I wish he'd talk to me a little more about those kinds of things."

"Give him time," replied Sarah.

"You're right," agreed Meg. "It really hasn't been very long. Honestly, when I think about everything that's happened in the past year, I'm amazed at how far he's come."

"How about Cindy's cafe?" asked Vicky.

"That would be perfect," replied Meg. "What do you think, Sarah?"

Sarah smiled. "I think Mum would love it, and we know the food would be good."

"It's settled then," replied Vicky. "We'll hold the baby shower at the Emerald Cafe, and we can see the beach from there so it's a win-win."

"I'll call Mum to see what dates she has free at the

cafe. She's pretty busy this time of year, but I'm sure we'll be able to find a date that suits."

* * *

CINDY

Darwin was hot. Cindy was used to hot weather, having spent all her life in northern New South Wales, a place known as the skin cancer capital of the world. Still, it had nothing on Darwin. They'd walked around the block together and picked up some ingredients to make dinner at the shop on the corner. Even though it was early evening, the heat hadn't dissipated.

"I had no idea it would be this hot," she said.

Adele laughed as she pulled the sliding door shut. Outside through the glass was a small balcony attached to Adele's unit; beyond the balcony sat a green park with a playground, another block of units beyond it.

"We're in the tropics, Mum, what did you think it'd be like?"

Cindy fanned her face with a one hand and moved to stand beneath the air conditioner as sweat made her clothing stick to her skin down her back and along her sides.

"I didn't think much about it. Although I'm certainly glad you have this air conditioner."

"Everyone has one in Darwin. Most people have swimming pools too. It's the only way we can survive."

"So, you like it up here?" Cindy wasn't sure how she was going to broach the subject of Adele moving back to the Cove. But ever since she'd arrived in Darwin the day before it'd played on her mind.

Adele was her youngest child, her baby. She couldn't stand by and watch her daughter fade away. Recent phone calls had her worried that Adele wasn't coping. Cindy still wasn't sure why; they hadn't spoken about anything important or deep since she arrived, only covering safer subjects like work, the gym, shopping and so on. Even so, she could see in Adele's eyes she wasn't happy, and it'd begun to take a toll on her health — she looked wan, thinner than usual, her features drawn, and her skin pale.

"I guess," replied Adele without any conviction.

The lacklustre response was jarring coming from her normally vivacious, passionate, and expressive daughter.

Adele pushed a strand of blond hair behind her ear then bent over the kitchen bench to slice a green apple into pieces.

"You hungry? I could make a banana cake, I know how much you love those." Cindy scurried into the kitchen, reaching for an apron that hung from the oven door handle.

"No, not really."

"Oh." She set the apron back on the door.

Adele offered her a half-hearted smile. "Sorry, Mum. You can make it if you want, I'm not really hungry."

"Have you seen the doctor lately?" she asked.

"Well, I told you I've been visiting a psychologist." Adele's cheeks pinked, her tone iced with irritation.

"I know, and I think that's great, but what if there's something physically wrong. I think it would be a good idea to get that checked out, you've lost a lot of weight."

Adele looked down at herself as though she'd never

noticed the weight loss before now. "Yeah, I suppose that's true."

"And you seem a lot less energetic than usual."

"I'm okay, Mum. I know you're worried about me, but really, I'll be fine. I'm not crazy or anything." Adele picked up a slice of apple and bit into it.

"I know you're not," countered Cindy. Nerves pooled in her gut. She was worried about Adele — she was a mother, no matter how old her child got. "Only, you don't really look yourself these days."

"Fine. I'll go to the doctor if it'll make you feel better."

Cindy sat primly on the edge of an armchair with her hands folded in her lap. "Thank you, it will help me to feel better. Do you want to talk about what's wrong?"

"Not really."

"Oh." She hadn't expected that. In fact, she'd flown all the way to Darwin with images running through her imagination of Adele opening up to her, hot tears streaming down her cheeks as Cindy wrapped her up in her arms and told her everything would be okay. In her mind, she'd be able to help her daughter through whatever was bothering her, convince her to move home, and all would be right with the world again. Of course, she knew Adele could be difficult to influence, but she'd always been open about how she was feeling, about what was going on in her life. It seemed this time might be different. She'd have to try another tack.

"But things are fine at work, are they?"

Adele shrugged. "I guess. They're having me fly more and more into Asia, which is exhausting. My schedule's all over the place. I'm hardly home, to be honest."

"I wish you'd come to the Cove — at least for a visit. It would do you some good to get out and have a swim in the ocean, to see your friends, have some home-cooked meals."

"I cook," objected Adele, sitting across from Cindy and pulling her knees up beside her on the two-seater blue couch.

"I mean *my* home cooking," replied Cindy with a chuckle.

"That does sound good."

"Perhaps you're worn out," offered Cindy, watching Adele closely. Were those dark patches beneath her eyes? Or perhaps her mascara had smudged.

"I'm tired, definitely. And—" Adele let out a heavy breath. "My boyfriend broke up with me."

Ah. It was all beginning to make some sense. She'd wondered if there was a man involved; it was strange for Adele to be so down when she was usually the first one in the family to laugh, see things from a positive perspective, play a prank, or tell a joke.

"I'm sorry, honey. That must've been difficult to deal with."

Adele's eyes misted over. "I still don't understand what happened. One minute he was telling me he loved me, that he wanted to spend his life with me. The next he's saying he can't see a future together."

"He didn't give you any other reason?" Cindy's nostrils flared. She'd like to have a word with this boyfriend, tell him exactly what she thought of him — rejecting her beautiful daughter that way. He'd clearly broken her heart and given her no reason for it. "You never told me about him. I didn't know you were seeing anyone." Cindy's brow furrowed. "Who is he?"

"I work with him, he's one of the pilots I fly with

on occasion. I didn't tell you about it because I didn't think you'd approve. He's older, in his thirties. Separated from his wife."

"Oh honey," said Cindy, her heart falling. "Separated? You're twenty-two years old. Far too young to be dating someone in his thirties. And separated means he's still married. I didn't raise you to—"

"I know, Mum," hissed Adele. She covered her face with both hands.

"Sorry. Of course you don't need me to talk about all that right now. Well, I'm glad it's over, even if it's been hard on you. Time to leave him behind in your rear vision mirror, my love." Cindy shifted over to the couch beside Adele and rested a hand on her daughter's shoulder. Adele moved closer, then snuggled into Cindy's side, one arm around Cindy's waist.

"I didn't mean to snap at you," she sniffled. "I know it was wrong, but he was so kind, so nice. It just happened."

"So, this is the reason you've been so upset?"

Adele nodded. "I can't get away from him, he's at work all the time, I run into him in the staff room, on flights. He calls me, texts me, I don't know what to do."

"Why is he calling you?" asked Cindy, anger stirring inside.

"I don't know, he likes to tell me he loves me and maybe we can still spend time together as friends."

"What? Uh-uh, I don't think so."

"Mum."

"You're going to have to trust my experience on this, honey. He's manipulating you."

Adele sat up straight, rubbed her nose with the back of her hand. "No, he cares about me. He's confused."

"Oh my darling, sometimes I forget how young you still are because you're a pilot and you fly all over the world. You're so amazing, and I'm prouder of you than I can say. But there's so much you have to learn about some things, men included. I wish you didn't have to learn the hard way and instead you'd take my advice — it's time to block his phone number, to ask work not to place you in the same plane as him, and to move on with your life."

Adele's mobile phone rang. She tugged it from her pocket and answered, her nose red and her eyes still blurred by tears.

"This is Adele."

Her eyes widened. "What? No. That can't be right. I don't know what you're talking about. I—"

She hung up the phone and stared at it as her lower lip trembled.

"Who was that?" asked Cindy.

Adele's teary gaze rose to meet hers. "I don't... I can't... she said she was his wife. That I'm a home wrecker, and she's going to tell everyone at work if I don't leave him alone. And then she called me some other names and hung up."

Cindy's throat tightened, her vision blurred. "Oh no." She pulled Adele into her arms, held her close. "Honey, I'm so sorry."

"I didn't know. He said he was separated."

"I know, honey. But separated means still married, and it's very likely he wasn't being truthful about any of it."

Adele pulled free of her embrace, studied her face. "You think he was lying?"

Cindy shrugged. "I'd bet money on it."

Adele buried her face in her hands, sobbing. Cindy

patted her back as her daughter cried, then padded into the small kitchen to boil the kettle. By the time she'd poured two cups of tea, set them on a tray with some chocolate biscuits and carried the tray back to the living room, Adele's tears had dried. She sat curled on the couch, staring out the windows at the park beyond.

Cindy set the tray on the coffee table and handed a cup to Adele.

"Thanks, Mum."

"You're welcome. I think it's time you came home. You need some space to sort all of this out."

"I can't run away from my problems. You taught me that."

"You're not running away," assured Cindy. "You're getting some perspective and fresh air. Two things I've also taught you."

Adele offered a sad smile. "Okay, I'll visit home. I've got some leave saved, and it'll be good to get away."

"You'll come?" Cindy's eyes widened. She'd prepared for an argument as Adele rarely gave in without a fight. She always had her own plan for every aspect of her life, and she'd been independent since the day she was born. Andy had joked she'd waltzed into their lives with one fist raised and a laugh that could rival the angels. He and Adele were as close as father and daughter could be. At least they had been before the divorce. Maybe some time with him would help her daughter recover from the heartbreak as well. It was certainly worth a try. They could all pitch in to help.

Adele sighed. "Yes, Mum. I'll come home. Other than Rupert's funeral and Sarah's wedding, I've hardly been home in years. It'd be nice to visit for no reason at all, other than to relax and spend time with you."

"Wonderful." Cindy's heart constricted at the look on her daughter's face. "We'll have fun, and you'll be able to put all of this behind you."

CHAPTER 18

BEN

*B*rown hair blinded Ben, covering his goggles as he turned his head to breathe. A small swell slapped against his face. He stopped swimming and tread water to give himself a chance to cough up the salt water and catch his breath.

He'd been living in the Cove for two weeks and decided it was time to get into a routine again. He'd unpacked everything and the house looked warm and welcoming. At least he thought so. Over the past few days he'd begun swimming in the ocean.

It wasn't something he'd ever tackled before. Living up north for most of his adult life he'd swum thousands of laps in cool pools alongside other lap swimmers, all tucked neatly into marked lanes. The ocean up north was full of deadly jellyfish and saltwater crocodiles. Not to mention the fact that in Townsville the tide retreated out of sight every afternoon, leaving behind ugly mud flats in its wake.

In contrast, the ocean in Emerald Cove was breathtaking. The sun glinted off its shifting surface as if a billion jewels hung there. Waves rolled to shore all day long, meeting the brilliant sand that reached long and white from one end of the Cove to the other in a sweeping curve.

The first day after he'd made the decision to get back into swimming, one of his life passions, he'd ridden his bike to the local swimming pool where a bevy of excited and energetic children splashed and played, making it difficult to find a lane. When two of the tykes tucked their legs and bombed into the pool right beside his lane, sending a wave of water directly into his mouth, he'd stood up, coughing and sputtering, and thought he might as well swim in the ocean.

The next day he did.

The sandy shore sparkled in the distance, about fifty metres away. It felt strange to be so far out, but he was slowly becoming accustomed to it. He had to get beyond the break to swim without being crushed by the waves, which sometimes meant he was a little further out in the bay than made him comfortable, but no doubt that feeling would fade with time.

With a kick, he pushed forward again, slowly getting back into a rhythm with his strokes. Long arms glided into the shimmering water while it rose and fell beneath him as if the ocean itself were sighing. Through his goggles he couldn't see much more than the deep green blue colour of the water with the occasional bubbles rising to the surface.

He was in decent shape. Not his best, but certainly not his worst either. Three weeks without exercise, during which time he'd packed up his entire life and moved to the Cove, was a long time for him. While spending time with his parents in Brisbane before the move he'd attended their local pool religiously. He also went on their regular evening walks with them. It'd been a special time as they'd chatted for hours on those walks.

He swam for another half an hour, arms moving in a steady rhythm, breath coming in deep, controlled gasps each time he cocked his head to one side.

Thoughts of Diana and Andy kept crossing his mind. Rupert's death had troubled him more than he'd realised. He'd met Rupert soon after his first visit to Emerald Cove in search of Diana. What short time he'd spent with the man had given him an impression of someone kind, patient and good. A man who hadn't deserved to be lied to for so long by the woman he loved.

Images of the man he'd never had the chance to get to know well traveled through his imagination. What if that'd been Diana, or Andy? He might never have had the chance to spend time with his birth parents. The thought gave him a sinking feeling.

The fact was, they were getting on in years. Neither one of them had reached out to him, looked for him, or as far as he could tell given him a second thought over the years. Diana said she thought about him every day, but what proof did he have of that? He wanted to give her the benefit of the doubt, to believe her words, but she'd lied to everyone in her life for almost forty-five years. How could he trust anything she said? Especially when her actions didn't back up her words.

If she really had thought of him often, cared about his wellbeing, wouldn't she have sought him out?

Looked for him to make some kind of connection? As it was, he might've missed the opportunity if he hadn't made the effort himself.

It wasn't Andy's fault, of course, as he hadn't even known Ben existed. But Diana knew. She didn't tell Andy he was a father, didn't let her friend Cindy know what'd happened, even though she had been married to Andy all those years. Hadn't even shared the secret with her beloved husband until Ben came to visit and forced the issue.

He hadn't let himself think about the whys: why didn't she want to keep him? Why didn't she care enough to tell anyone in her life about him, or to search for him? Even now, it was usually him who called her to talk. Perhaps he'd misread this entire situation and she didn't want to see him or spend time with him as much as he'd believed she did.

He swam to shore and strode from the ocean, salt-water running down his body. With a grunt, he pushed the goggles up onto his forehead and rubbed his reddened eyes with his fingertips. Swimming in the ocean gave him a thrill every time he did it. There was a challenge to it, a thrill of danger that he didn't feel when he swam laps in an enclosed pool. He emerged feeling as though nothing could stop him, he could conquer the world. And usually, there was a peace that washed over him, having worked through the thoughts in his head as he swam. But not today. Today, his body buzzed with anger.

He rode his bike back to the rental house, showered under the external shower head beside the house and dried off with the towel he'd hung there.

Inside, he sat at the kitchen table and reached for his mobile phone. He dialled his parents' house, then waited as the phone rang. It rang so long he began to get worried, then his mother's voice said his name. A sweet sound that filled him with warmth.

"Mum, how are you?"

He could hear the smile on her words. "Oh, I'm pretty good today, thanks, honey. How about you?"

"I'm good. Just got back from my swim."

"Oh yeah? I worry about you, swimming in the ocean like that. Are you sure it's safe?"

"Yes, I'm fine. I don't want you to worry. I called because I miss you and Dad."

"That's so lovely to hear. We miss you as well. Is everything okay down there?"

He rubbed a hand over his face, sighed. "Yeah, it's fine. Only, I don't know many people in town yet. I forgot how hard it is, and how long it takes, to get established in a new place. I guess it's going to be a while before I make friends and feel at home here."

"That's true, honey. It's a long process. That's why I was so worried about you starting out all over again in a new town on your own." She'd objected to the move at first, but had backed down when he told her it was something he felt he had to do.

"How about this — I promise if it gets too hard, or it doesn't work out, I'll be back in Brisbane in the blink of an eye."

She laughed. "Okay, I'll hold you to that."

* * *

FRANKLIN

With sweat still beading across his brow from the run he'd taken from his house to the station, Franklin stood from behind his desk and strode into the common area. He'd spent the past ten days working and visiting the hospital, and not much else. His father's condition was stable, but he hadn't improved much either. Franklin worried about him constantly, but he also had a police station to run and the stress of it all sometimes overwhelmed him. Running helped ease the tension, but then he stayed hot for the rest of the day even after a cold shower.

"Is this air-conditioning on?" he bellowed to no one in particular.

Bec spun in her chair to face him, one eyebrow quirked. "I think so, boss. Everything okay?"

He swiped at the sweat on his forehead. "Everything's fine, only it feels like an oven in here."

She shrugged. "Feels okay to me."

He found the control panel on the wall, studied it with his hands pressed to his hips. Why did the confounded thing have to be so confusing? He swipe a hand in front of a glass panel, then pressed buttons and nothing happened. It drove him mad the way he was expected to be some kind of rocket scientist just to manage the air temperature in his police station.

He jabbed at a button again, and the entire station fell into darkness.

"Uh, boss?" Bec's voice travelled to him with a hint of laughter.

It only irritated him further.

"Bloody space-craft nonsense," he muttered, as Steph burst through the door from reception. He couldn't see her but heard the door and knew what her face would look like — brow furrowed, eyes wide.

"Everyone okay?" she called.

He grunted again. "We're all fine, I'm trying to

operate this stupid air conditioning so it doesn't feel like I'm working in a furnace."

Within a few moments, Steph was beside him. She swiped and tapped at the control panel and the lights flickered back to life. Steph smiled at him.

"Huh, thanks," he said. "It doesn't like me."

She rolled her eyes and resumed tapping. "It likes you fine, you've simply got to learn how to use it."

"It should be intuitive. It's not user friendly, and that isn't my fault."

"Okay, well I've turned the temp down. Now hopefully we don't all freeze into solid blocks of ice at our desks."

Franklin headed for his office, stopping at the door when he saw Nicole leaning against his door frame in an aqua halter top and denim shorts. Her long, tanned arms were crossed over her chest, a smile played at the corner of her mouth.

"What's going on in here? Having some trouble with the lights?"

He shrugged then combed fingers through his hair. "Nothing I can't handle. What are you doing here?"

Her smile drooped. "I came to see you. Thought we might grab some lunch later."

She sauntered into his office. He followed her and shut the door behind them. The last thing he needed was for Bec and Steph to overhear their conversation. He wouldn't be surprised if he came out and found Steph's ear glued to the other side of the door; that woman seemed to know everything going on in the office and in his life without him saying a word — he'd never been able to figure how she managed it.

He sat at his desk, steepled his fingers, and studied Nicole. Even after all these years she still carried the same smirk on her face she'd had when they were kids. He knew her well enough to understand it was a mask — she wasn't so self-assured as she played. She'd learned to put on a brave front, especially when she was nervous. And she was doing it now. Only he wasn't certain why.

She sat in the chair opposite him then crossed one lean leg over the other.

"So, what's up buttercup?" she asked, with a chuckle.

"Is there something going on with you I don't know about?" he asked.

Her eyes narrowed. "What do you mean?"

"I mean, I know you well enough that I can see when you're hiding something. You're upset or anxious, so something's going on with you. Do you want to talk about it?"

The mask fell. "You can tell, huh?"

He nodded, sighed. "Of course I can. I'm worried about you, but I also wonder why you're back in the Cove and coming to see me in my office. You left me, if you remember, and walked away. You didn't want me in your life — you told me that in no uncertain terms. I wasn't *enough* for you. I believe those were your exact words."

Nicole shook her head slowly. "I'm sorry I said that, it was mean and not true."

"It is what it is." He leaned back in his chair, nostrils flared.

"I can tell you're still angry with me about it."

"No, not angry, not anymore. I was for a long time. But you and I weren't right for each other and I figured that out eventually. I'm only sorry it ended the way it did. I don't hold it against you, Nic."

"But you're not willing to give us another chance." Her voice faded, her countenance written with resignation.

Franklin sighed. "No, I'm sorry. I can't do that, but I hope we can be friends and see each other more than once every five years."

"That sounds nice."

"So, you're okay?"

"I think I'm going through a mid-life crisis or something."

He quirked an eyebrow. "You're not that old."

"I was always precocious," she replied with a wink.

He laughed. "That is very true."

"Thanks for asking, I'm fine, I missed home. And since none of my family lives here anymore, I've had no excuse to visit. When I think of home, of the Cove, I think of you." She stood, rubbing her palms down the front of her shorts. "I shouldn't have left the way I did, but there was this itch inside of me — I had to leave, to experience something of the world. After my parents divorced and moved away, something inside of me shifted — I couldn't be here anymore."

He walked over to kiss her cheek. "Thank you for the apology the other night, and the explanation now. It's not necessary — not anymore — but it's appreciated."

"I never stopped caring about you."

He squeezed her shoulder. "Me too."

He walked her out to the reception area. She turned to face him, her eyes glistening. "I guess I'll see you around."

With a nod, he closed his arms around her, feeling the comfort of her familiarity, the love they'd shared for so many years that was now laced with a happy nostalgia. She hugged him back, then waved goodbye as she left.

He was glad she'd come back to the Cove. Glad she'd sought him out to talk — even if he wasn't able to give her what she wanted. There was no way it would've worked between them, but he'd always care for her. She was his oldest friend from those carefree days running wild around town with bare feet and a surfboard tucked beneath his arm.

He shoved his hands deep into his pockets and swung around to walk back into the office. Bec stood by the reception desk in her navy uniform, hair pulled neatly into a low ponytail. She was deep in conversation with Steph, discussing something in a manila folder. He offered her a nod.

She set the folder down on the desk and strode towards him, her hands clenched at her sides. He stopped, blinked.

"So, are you two getting married?"

His brow furrowed. "What?"

"Well, you were engaged. So, if you're back together, I'm assuming it's all back on."

Franklin's mouth fell open. What was she talking about? Why would anyone think he and Nicole were engaged?

"So?" she asked, her foot tapping a rapid beat on the tiled floor.

"Bec, you don't understand."

"You're right, I don't. You're so hot and cold, all over the place. One minute, you're warm and caring, the next you're grumpy and closed off. One day you're single, the next you're engaged to a woman who left five years ago and then showed up out of the blue. A woman who seems to me to be completely opposite to you in every way. I don't understand you at all, Franklin."

"I don't know what to say to that, Proby. Perhaps you've gotten some wires crossed."

Anger flared red in her cheeks. "Don't be patronising. You've got to make some decisions about what you want in life, and who you want to spend that life with."

"I suppose that's true." He was so confused. She was talking about Nicole. Right? But it sounded like she meant something other than what she was saying, which was exactly the kind of thing he was usually really good at interpreting — he could figure out the meaning behind the words of every criminal he'd ever interviewed. But Bec was another matter entirely. "I thought things between us were good but you seem upset."

"It's like you're the incarnation of Sherlock Holmes," she hissed, shaking her head.

"Proby..."

She raised both hands, as if in surrender. "No, forget it. You're right, I'm the Proby, you're the boss. It's none of my business what you do in your personal life, or who you choose to spend that life with. Nothing to do with me, whatsoever."

With a toss of her head, she stormed through the glass sliding doors and out into the street. Franklin watched her go, his eyes narrowed, his thoughts in a whirl. What was going on with her today? She'd seemed fine earlier.

With a sigh, he tugged his hands from his pockets, and rubbed them over his face. "These women will be the death of me."

Steph huffed.

He glanced at her — round peaches and cream complexion with pink cheeks, red curls tumbling around her face. Her green eyes flashed.

"Franklin Russell, sometimes you're the smartest guy in the room. Other times, you're just plain clueless."

CHAPTER 19

REBECCA

*T*he boxing bag shuddered as Rebecca showered it with punches. A left upper cut, then a right, followed by a left hook. Then a volley of body shots in rapid succession.

Her breathing laboured, she grunted as she landed the final blow. Then stood, heaving for breath, her shoulders hunched.

The gym was empty, the class long over. Drab blue carpet, buckets of soiled inner gloves ready for washing, black and red boxing gloves in piles — it was all so familiar to her, so comforting. She loved it there, the workout, the power she felt from it, the people who'd become friends.

Everyone else from the boxing class had wandered outside chatting or headed for the showers. Rebecca remained behind, determined to get some more time in — she'd missed so much recovering from all of her injuries. The break had healed well, but her right hand still twinged if she hit the bag too hard, even though she'd strapped it more carefully than her left. So, she held back, not giving it her all when driving with her right but making up for it with her left hand — giving every punch the full impact of her strength and weight.

She gulped a mouthful of water, then stepped back to the bag, easing her head to one side, then the other, to stretch the tense muscles in her neck. She jogged a little in place, one foot to the other, then punched — this time, with less vigour and more focus on technique. Jab, jab, jab, dance to the right, jab, dance to the left, jab.

The thoughts rushed back, bringing with them a pang of regret that swirled in her gut. Why had she said those things to Franklin? She'd had no intention of confronting him that way, but when she saw him embrace his fiancée, or former fiancée, whatever Nicole was to him, she'd felt a sudden rush of jealousy, anger, frustration — a swirl of emotions she hadn't been ready for and that'd pushed her to react in a way she was embarrassed to recall.

He was her employer, her boss, her partner. Not to mention the fact that he was dealing with his father's ill health and daily visits to the hospital. And she'd shouted at him in the office, where they worked together, about his love life. What was she thinking?

Remembering the look on his face brought a fresh wave of shame that made her hands drop to her sides as she puffed hard from the exertion.

"You okay?" asked Elise, the new trainer who'd taken over the class in recent weeks but had already become a fast friend. She walked to the wall, stacking boxing pads in a corner.

Rebecca sighed and removed her gloves. "Yeah, I guess so. I made a fool of myself today at the station."

"Oh yeah?" Elise studied her with eyebrows arched.

Rebecca walked over to Elise and handed her the gloves. "I usually bring my own but I didn't intend to come to the class this evening. I just had a few things to work out in my head."

Elise added the gloves to the pile. "No worries, I'm glad you came. Anything you want to talk about?"

"I shouted at my boss." Rebecca rubbed her hands over her face with a groan. "I embarrassed myself, and him. He was so confused, I was mortified. Ugh, I hate even thinking about it. Besides that, his dad is in hospital, so I know he's worried about that, and now I've added to his stress."

"Oh wow, I'm sorry. What did you yell at him about?"

Rebecca grimaced. It was embarrassing to even say the words. "His ex-fiancée is back in town and, well, I know it's stupid but I thought he and I shared a moment, a few moments really. We were in a good place, things were progressing."

"You want to be more than friends and colleagues with him," said Elise, her blond ponytail bobbing as she nodded.

Rebecca sighed. "I don't know exactly. Yes, I suppose that's true, although I hadn't really thought it through completely. It's a terrible idea, dating a colleague, so it's probably for the best."

"Do you really think so?"

She laughed. "No, I don't. But she's back in town, and it looks as though everything's back on between them, that's what people are saying, anyway. I've been helping him with his dad, bringing meals to the hospital, visiting. We've had some really special times, some good talks, and I haven't seen her anywhere — she's left him to deal with it alone as far as I can tell. And then, this morning I saw them hugging, and something inside me just snapped. I told him he needed to make a decision about who he wanted to spend his life with. Can you believe it?" She covered her face with both hands. "And now he probably thinks I'm a crazy person — well, even more than he already did."

"I don't know, that doesn't sound too crazy to me. Besides, from what you've told me about your past, I wouldn't be surprised if you have trust issues. It's going to be hard for you to form a relationship with a man again after everything you've been through. You're attracted to your boss, but you're scared to admit it to yourself or to take the next step."

It made sense. She hadn't made good decisions in the past about romantic relationships. How could she trust herself to be sensible now? She had to question everything she felt and couldn't put her faith in those feelings. Every time she thought about Franklin in a romantic light, something pushed her to the verge of panic, and perhaps that's why she'd reacted the way she had.

"You think I'm pushing him away intentionally?"

"Maybe," admitted Elise. "It's definitely something to think about. Is this man…"

"Franklin."

"Right, Franklin. Is he a good man?"

Rebecca's lips pursed. "The best."

"Do you care for him?"

She nodded, the words sticking in her throat.

"Do you think he cares for you in the same way?"

"I don't know. There've been moments when it seemed like he might. But he's very difficult to read."

"You have to remember, he's your boss so he's probably trying hard to keep things professional and not misread any signals from you. And if you're giving him mixed signals…"

"Looking back I think I can say with certainty, that I definitely have. I mean, not intentionally. But I've kept my distance most of the time, haven't really given him any indication of how I feel. I suppose he doesn't know."

Elise shrugged. "Seems likely he's completely in the dark. So, if he's renewing a relationship with his ex, you can't look at that as a rejection for you personally, since I doubt he knows how you feel about him."

"Do you think I should tell him?" The thought brought a flutter of nerves into Rebecca's chest.

"I think you should, but you'll have to pick the right time — I mean, he is your boss. That complicates things."

"It definitely does. If he doesn't feel the same way, things will be awkward between us. It'll change everything."

"So, maybe think about it," suggested Elise.

"I'm going to spend Christmas with my family in Sydney, maybe when I get back I'll have an opportunity to talk to him about it. He's got so much on his plate at the moment, with Nicole in town and his father in the hospital."

Elise smiled, tossed a towel over her shoulder. "Sounds like a plan. I'll see you tomorrow."

She waved a hand over her head as she left, and Rebecca headed for the parking lot. She didn't have a towel or change of clothes with her and had only thrown on leggings and a shirt that she'd kept in the car. She'd have to shower at home.

Everything Elise said made a lot of sense. All she had to do now was figure out if she wanted to risk losing the good working relationship she and Franklin shared, for the possibility of something more.

CHAPTER 20

MEG

*P*ink bunting hung from the cafe walls, while pink balloons swung gently in the breeze that came off the beach and whistled through The Emerald Cafe's outdoor eating area. Meg linked her hands together behind her back, her fingers twisting, then pulled them apart, and rubbed her swollen belly.

Guests had begun to arrive at her baby shower, and she was welcoming them one by one, but nerves churned in the pit of her gut. She wasn't accustomed to being the centre of attention. Brad had disappeared a few minutes after they'd arrived, and everyone wanted to know where he was. Now she had to put on a smile and accept congratulations knowing there might well be something very wrong with her baby.

Vicky linked an arm through Meg's. "You look beautiful, Meg," she whispered.

Meg offered her a half smile. "I look like a gigantic hippo."

"No," Vicky laughed. "You look amazing. If I look half as wonderful as you when I'm pregnant, I'll be a happy woman."

Meg sighed and did her best to let the tension drift from her neck and shoulders. Sarah and Vicky had put the party together for her, so she couldn't be ungrateful. After all, she'd never had friends like this before — friends who would do something so special, who would celebrate her this way.

Sarah joined them and handed Meg a glass of punch. The three of them clinked glasses. "Cheers!"

They drank. Meg's gaze wandered around the cafe. Where was Brad? He was supposed to be here. He'd promised her he would be part of the event. Some of his friends had already arrived. She'd wanted this to be an event they celebrated together.

"Are you looking for Brad?" asked Sarah.

She nodded, chewing on her lower lip.

"I think I saw him go outside."

"Really?" She couldn't imagine where he'd gone. But she wasn't his mother or his keeper. If he wanted to be difficult there was nothing she could do about it. She pushed thoughts of Brad out of her mind. He could take care of himself. "Thank you for putting this together. I really appreciate both of you."

Sarah grinned. "We were happy to do it. You're going to be a wonderful mother."

The words tore at something inside Meg. Would she? Her fear was that she'd become like her own mother, that one day her child would move as far away as she could only to get away from Meg. Meg would do everything in her power to be a different parent than her own had been, but what if it wasn't enough?

Brad wheeled into the café and smiled across the room at Meg. Relief washed over her. She hurried to join him.

"Are you all right?"

He nodded. "Fine. Let's mingle."

They spent the next two hours chatting with guests, eating, and drinking. By the time the shower was over, Meg's feet ached, her back was sore, and she really needed to sit. She found a chair and put her feet up on another while Brad finished loading the gifts they'd opened into the back of their car. She was constantly amazed by how independent he'd become; he'd seemed happy and engaged throughout the entire party.

Finally, he joined her, took her bare feet into his hands, and massaged them one by one. The gesture brought a tear to her eye. It'd been so long since he'd been tender and caring. These days she generally felt as though she was the care giver, and he would receive everything she had to give without offering much in return. It was hard enough for him to tackle each day between his studies, the commute to and from university, and the internship. She knew it all took a toll on him and when he came home in the evenings, he often didn't have anything left to give.

"Thank you for being here today," she said.

He shrugged. "I'm excited about the baby, and it was fun."

Her throat tightened. "Hearing that makes me very happy." She didn't want to talk to him about her fears. Not today. Today was a happy day, a day to celebrate their daughter's life and Meg's pregnancy with family

173

and friends. Discussions about what the future might hold for their precious child could wait for another day.

He smiled and set her feet back on the chair. "Let's go home."

She drove them home but when they climbed out of the car in the underground garage, Brad sat staring at their locker. Each unit had one made of black wire mesh with a padlock on the door. Most stored bicycles or scooters and there were even a few jet skis. But only one held a custom-made beach-ready wheelchair.

"I'd like to go down to the beach. If you have the energy," he said, suddenly.

The sand was cold on her feet. Her stomach was so big now that she felt a little off kilter all of the time. Trudging through soft, white sand made her puff hard after only a few steps, especially pushing the wheelchair ahead of her. But nothing could dampen her spirits. Brad wanted to visit the beach, and she'd do anything to make it happen.

The sun had already set behind them, only a glow on the horizon announced its location. The ocean rolled black beyond the sand. A jogger plodded by. A family hurried towards the parking lot, dropping sand toys and towels then rushing back to pick them up as they went.

"The beach smells so good," said Brad in a wistful voice.

"I love it here. I know it's been hard for you but living across from the beach has saved me this year. I've spent a lot of hours sitting here on the sand, or swimming in the water."

"Really?" Brad spun to face her with one eyebrow quirked. "I didn't know that."

"I didn't tell you," she said with a soft voice as she caressed his cheek.

A muscle in his jaw clenched. "I know I haven't been easy to live with this year."

"Let's not talk about that," she replied. "Let's enjoy this beautiful evening. It's a good day today, I only want to talk about good things."

Once on the harder sand, Brad was able to wheel himself a little. He spun around, even reached down to touch the expended wave, then threw the water at Meg. She squealed and ran out of his reach then splashed him back, making him laugh out loud.

She ended up seated in his lap as the two of them watched the moon rise together over the ocean. It was almost full. Bright and glowing it settled in the inky sky, soon surrounded by glinting stars.

"I'm not too heavy?" asked Meg, leaning back into Brad.

He sighed. "No, you're perfect."

He rested a hand on her belly. She snuggled closer, her head pressing into the space beneath his chin — the place she always felt safest.

"I've been so worried," she began.

He shushed her. "I thought we were only going to talk about good things."

"I know, but it *is* good — I feel so much relief." Tears blurred her vision. "We're really going to be okay. Aren't we?"

He kissed the top of her head, stroked her hair. "As long as we have each other, we'll manage whatever comes our way."

CHAPTER 21

FRANKLIN

*I*t happened quickly. Even though Franklin knew his father was unwell, he'd had two strokes for heaven's sake, he still wasn't ready for it when the phone call came in the middle of the night.

Dad was gone. He died peacefully, while sleeping. Franklin supposed he couldn't ask for more than that. And they'd had a lot of good years together. Not as many as they should've had, but there wasn't anything to be done about that now.

That was the hardest part about this whole thing. He had no control over it. None at all. He couldn't bark at someone that they had no right to take his father yet, couldn't order his father to comply, couldn't charge anyone with anything to make it all stop. Death came, it took whoever it had its sights on, and those left behind had to live with it.

What else was there to do?

He sat on his bed, head in his hands, grief sucking the breath from his lungs. He'd rushed to the hospital, cried over his father's body, said his goodbyes, filled out every piece of paperwork the kind nurse in the blue scrubs had shoved under his nose. And now he was at home, wondering what on earth he should do.

Sleep. He should probably sleep. But there was no way he was going to be able to get back to sleep now. Besides, it was four a.m., and the sun was on its way. Birds would soon set up a morning chorus. It was almost summer and dawn was arriving earlier and earlier each day.

If he weren't going to sleep, maybe he should get up and do something. But what?

What he really wanted to do was talk to someone. Not someone. Bec. He needed to hear her voice that was all. Perhaps she wouldn't mind if he called early. From what he understood she was usually an early riser — she often went to a class at the boxing gym before she came to the station.

He reached for the telephone on the bedside table and dialled. She answered with a sleep-soaked voice.

"Hello?"

"I'm sorry, I know it's early, but I wanted to talk to you."

"Boss?"

He pinched the bridge of his nose. "Yeah, it's me."

The grogginess disappeared in a flash. "What's wrong? What happened. Do you need me at the station?"

"No, no, nothing like that. I wanted to hear your voice."

"Okay, where are you?"

Grief speared his chest. "I'm at home."

"I'm coming over."

He shook his head in the darkness. "No, you don't have to do that."

"What's going on, Franklin?" She rarely used his name — usually calling him boss, or Sarge, or any number of other nicknames, the same everyone in the office used to talk about him behind his back. Not that he minded. Still, it was nice to hear his name on her lips.

"Dad died."

"I'm so sorry."

"Thanks." Tears gathered in his throat. "It was sudden. I thought he was getting better."

"I'll be there in a few minutes. Half an hour tops," she said.

He didn't have the strength to object. He didn't want her to feel obligated, but he really did want her there. She owed him nothing but having her here would help. He knew it, without even having to form the thought.

"Okay. It's Pelican Way…"

"I know where you live, boss," she said, her voice warm.

He boiled the kettle three times while he waited. Every time he looked away from the window where the sun was rising and colouring the sky like an artist with a paintbrush, and stared at the kettle, he had a sudden realisation that he'd forgotten to pour a cup of tea and the water had cooled. He hated cool tea, preferred it scalding hot. Steph said he had a tongue of iron, since whenever she made him a cup, he asked her not to add milk or cold water.

One of the few things he'd inherited from his mother. Or at least he thought he remembered that

179

about her; she drank tea so hot it would give a person third degree burns if it spilled. He recalled Dad saying something to that effect one time when they were talking about her and he'd said he couldn't remember much. He'd been upset that his recollections of her, the pictures in his mind, the piecemeal memories of things they'd done, or what she'd said, were all fading. Soon, he'd have nothing left of her but her wedding ring and a quilt she'd stitched together out of his baby clothes.

Dad was always good at reminding him about the things he'd forgotten — the little things that didn't really matter, but when they were all added together formed a patchwork of memories that gave him a warm feeling inside whenever he thought about it.

A knock at the door startled him from his reverie. He strode to answer it. Rebecca stood in the bungalow's doorway holding a Tupperware container and two cups of coffee with steam rising from the lids.

"I brought coffee and breakfast. I wasn't sure if you like English muffins, but I grilled some with ham and cheese," she said.

He stepped aside and waved a hand towards the kitchen. "Wow, thanks. I was attempting to make us tea, but I hadn't managed it yet. So this is perfect. Come on in."

She set everything on his kitchen table, studying him with worried eyes as he crossed the room.

"Can I get you anything? Water, napkins?" he asked.

She shook her head. "No, Franklin, I'm fine. Are you okay?"

Was he okay? No, was the simple answer. Would he ever be again? He had no family left in the world other than a few distant cousins he never saw. His best friend was gone. His fiancée had left him years earlier. He'd never felt so alone.

"Uh." What could he say? He wasn't accustomed to pity, but that was the look she gave him now. He'd probably get a lot of that for a few days, weeks maybe. Then, everything would go back to normal, except he'd still be an island in the midst of a sweeping ocean.

She closed the gap between them and wrapped her arms around him in a warm embrace. Her head pressed to his chest, her arms around his torso, she mumbled into his shirt.

"I'm so sorry, Franklin."

THE NEXT FEW days were a blur to Franklin. As much as he realised in retrospect he should've prepared for this event, he hadn't done it. He didn't know who to invite to the funeral, what music to play, who should speak, where the old photographs were hidden - in his father's closet at the house or in the storage facility he'd rented when he sold his home and moved in with Franklin.

There were phone calls to make, people to tell, an obituary to write, casseroles to find homes for once his fridge was packed to the brim. He wouldn't have managed if it weren't for Bec and Steph. Both women bolstered him, encouraged him, and took on whatever tasks they were able.

When Steph went home to be with her family, it was Bec who remained behind to make sure he ate, or to help proofread the few paragraphs the local newspaper had agreed to run.

Peter Russell had lived in Emerald Cove all his life.

There were a lot of people who'd want to know about his passing, and to say farewell.

They held the funeral at the local Baptist church, a small building made of red brick, with a modest steeple and white trim. Peter had been a parishioner there for as long as Franklin could remember — in fact, he was fairly certain his grandparents had attended and taken Peter along with them when the church was brand new.

The only thing he could focus on during the service was the large black and white photograph of his father he'd had printed on canvas and set on a stand in the centre of the stage. He worked hard to control his emotions. The last thing he wanted was to put on a show for everyone in the building. He was a private man, and he hated to let others know how he was feeling.

Bec sat a few rows back with the rest of the team from the station. He wished she were beside him, instead of a great-aunt he hadn't seen since he was five years old. He could've squeezed her hand and perhaps things wouldn't seem quite so miserable, at least for a moment.

Everything said about his father, by friends, neighbours and distant relatives, was true. He was a good man, loved by many, and always willing to lend a hand. Quiet and reserved but kind to all. Sometimes abrupt but happy to apologise if his words caused any pain. With a heart as big as the ocean he'd loved and swum in until he could no longer manage to stand when a wave washed to shore.

When he'd stopped swimming — because the water was too bloody cold as he'd told Franklin — he'd taken to walking along the beach for kilometres each day. In his final years, he'd sat on bench seats that overlooked the ocean, watching the waves roll in and suck back out into its blue depths.

The ache in Franklin's chest made it hard to breathe. He'd miss his father so much he wasn't sure how he'd manage. Who could he talk to now about whatever was on his mind? There were people in his life who cared about him, he knew that, but he wasn't open with them about his struggles and fears the way he'd been with his father. He couldn't be — he was the cop in charge, the one who kept the community safe at night. He had a responsibility to be strong.

After the service, they held a wake in the hall behind the church. He hadn't wanted to hold it at his house, since he couldn't bear the thought of everyone there — sitting in Dad's chair, sipping from Dad's favourite teacup. And he wanted to be able to slip out when he'd had enough.

He stayed as long as he could then left when the sun settled beyond the horizon, casting long shadows from the tip of the church roof across the parking lot.

The drive home was quiet. Too quiet. He flicked on the radio and listened for a moment, but the music was too chipper for his mood, so he turned it off again.

At home, the house sat in solemn silence, dark and stifling in the humid air. He turned on a few lights, then loosened his tie and climbed out of his clothes. Selecting some soft gym shorts and a T-shirt with a hole near the neck, then he settled on the couch and switched on the tv.

When there was a knock at the door, he muted the television and glared at the door as if that might make the person go away. He didn't want visitors tonight. Not now. He couldn't take one more well-wisher, as much as he'd loved hearing the way his dad had touched their lives. It would push him over the edge into a full-blown bawling fest. And even though he was sure a psychologist would tell him that crying was good and that he shouldn't avoid his feelings, right now all he wanted to do was push those feelings down and watch some television. He could process his grief later. There'd been too much emotion already today and he was spent.

The person at the door knocked again, this time a little louder, and it was clear to Franklin they weren't going anywhere. With a sigh, he ambled to the door and flung it open, hoping a frown would chase whoever it was away in short order.

Bec offered him a half-grin, held up a bottle of wine and a brown paper bag containing something that smelled deliciously like freshly baked bread.

"I come bearing gifts," she said, leaning against the door frame, her dark hair mussed and falling across one cheek partially obscuring one deep brown eye.

Franklin's heart swelled with love for this woman who'd had so much thrown at her but remained the most kind, caring and thoughtful person he knew. The fact that she was sexy as heck was a bonus in his mind. Besides that, his father had adored her and told him as much on more than one occasion.

"Frankie, boy, you've got to take the time to see what's right in front of you," he'd said one day when they were in the middle of a particularly frustrating game of Scrabble.

Frustrating for Franklin, since he had managed to collect a bunch of letters that were completely useless, while he watched his father get a triple word score with 'ghee', of all unlikely things.

He'd shaken his head, one hand caressing the stubble on his chin from two days of not shaving while off work. "How the heck do you know what ghee is, Dad? You barely eat anything other than lamb chops and overdone veggies for dinner. And I can't remember the last time I saw you cook."

Dad had chuckled at that. "You're not listening, son. I'm talking about that delightful partner of yours, who, by the way, has clearly got her sights set on you. And that makes you the luckiest man in the world, in my opinion."

Franklin had looked up at that, caught the twinkle in his dad's eye. "What? No, not Bec. She works for me, it's not like that."

"You're a fool," replied Dad with a tssk of the tongue.

The memory of that night washed over Franklin, bringing a tightness to his throat that made his voice hoarse.

"I don't know what to say."

"How about 'come in'?" she offered with a laugh.

"Come in," he replied. "And thank you. I don't know how you do it."

"What's that?" She set the wine and bag on the table, then rooted around in a kitchen cupboard for a moment before extracting a white china plate.

"You seem to know exactly what I need, just when I need it."

She grinned, pulled a sticky bun out of the bag, and set it on the plate. Custard oozed from one side of the bun.

"There's nothing I can do to help you feel better," she said. "But wine and a piece of sticky bun are always welcome. Right?"

He nodded, leaning against the wall beside the table to watch her, arms crossed over his chest.

She cut the bun into pieces, poured two glasses of wine, then spun to face him. The smile on her face faded as she drank him in, her brown eyes darkening. She shook her head and reached out one hand to cup his cheek. He leaned into her hand, his heart thundering against his ribcage. She smelled of lilac and soap, just like always. He'd breathed in that scent almost every single day for an entire year every time she rode in the cruiser beside him or came into his office for a meeting.

Dad was right. He'd been a fool.

He took a step towards her, then another and swept her up into his arms, pressing his lips to hers in a passionate kiss that set his pulse racing. She relaxed in his arms and kissed him back, winding her arms around his neck and standing on tiptoe to pull him closer.

CHAPTER 22

CINDY

"I know you're glad to have Adele at home again, even if it is only for a little while," said Diana, taking a sip of green tea from a delicate china cup, hand painted with roses that Cindy had picked up at a sale a decade earlier. She couldn't recall exactly where, but she loved the china; a few pieces of the set had broken over the years, but most remained in good shape. She'd even found a few replacement pieces on eBay, which had been most satisfying.

"I'm over the moon," she said, pushing the plate of scones lavishly coated with jam and cream in Diana's direction.

Diana waved a hand, her brow furrowed. "No thank you, I couldn't possibly have another. I'm sure Ethan will finish those off for you."

"I miss having him living here."

"I'm sure you do. But what perfect timing to have

Adele home," replied Diana with a smile, before finishing her tea.

"I know. It's silly, but I miss having the house filled with their noise. When they all lived here, I couldn't help longing for a moment's peace and now I have all the peace I could want, and I hate it." She laughed and set her cup down on the tray between them.

The garden fairly hummed with the sound of bees and the chatter and titter of birds that flitted around the flower beds and bushes. The climbing roses that wound around the verandah posts were in full bloom, pink and succulent, their scent filling the air.

"Do you really hate it?" asked Diana.

"I suppose that's not entirely fair. Only, I expected I'd at least have a husband living with me when the children moved out. Now look at me — apart from Adele's visit, it's only Petal and me."

Diana set her cup down as well, smoothed her skirt with one hand, her countenance serious. "You're definitely selling then?"

"You know I've talked about it before. But this time, I think I'm ready."

"Well, it does make sense. I hated to part with Seaside Manor, but in the end, it was for the best."

Diana's lips pursed and her eyes misted. Cindy knew she was thinking of her late husband, Rupert, and wishing they'd moved out of the bed and breakfast years earlier so the two of them could've enjoyed retirement together. But they'd already talked over the subject a number of times, with Diana sobbing her heart out in Cindy's arms, so there was no need to raise it again. It'd only cause Diana more pain.

Diana left a few minutes later. The sun was setting behind the house across the street, and Cindy decided it was the perfect time to get some gardening done. Adele had gone out to dinner with Emily — they had a lot to catch up on since their last visit — so Cindy was on her own. She'd probably heat up some beans on toast, or a can of soup. It was hard to muster the motivation to cook an entire meal for one person after working all day at the cafe.

Adele had suggested she take some time off, but after a week in Darwin she had to get on top of things before she took more time for herself. Although it was important to make sure Adele had plenty of her attention, or as much as Adele wanted anyway. It was always a balancing act for her now her children were adults — how much of her attention did they want or need? She did her best to give them plenty without overdoing it so they could have time to themselves when they visited.

She slipped on a pair of gardening gloves, reached for her secateurs, a small trowel, and a kneeling cushion, then headed for the bed nearest the chook pen — it hadn't been weeded in a long time and there was a rogue cherry tomato plant overtaking her pansies. It must've seeded from her compost, since she'd never have planted it amongst her flowers but instead in the vegetable garden which she'd neglected for the better part of five years now.

She kneeled on the cushion and plucked weeds from the ground, while humming the tunes she'd heard on the radio earlier that day. The heat of the day dissipated slowly as the sun dipped beyond the horizon and the ocean breeze picked up.

"I should've known you'd be gardening, although I hope you know it's practically pitch dark out here." Andy's voice startled her from her reverie.

She staggered to her feet, brushed off her knees and studied him with a smile. "Well, isn't this a surprise?"

* * *

ANDY SAT on the back porch, one leg crossed over the other and a glass of iced tea in his hand, staring out over the garden. Cindy had strung twinkle lights in some of the small trees and the garden looked like a wonderland — she didn't think she'd ever tire of that view.

She'd showered and thrown together a light meal of whatever finger foods she could find in the fridge for the two of them after he'd asked if they could talk. It sounded ominous, so she decided food would help — there was no way she could face a serious conversation on an empty stomach and remain patient and kind, the way she'd vowed she would when dealing with Andy or Keisha since they moved back to town.

She set the tray of food on the table, hurried back to the kitchen for her own glass of tea, and then settled into a seat across from him.

"This is a little unusual," she began, offering him an opening to raise whatever it was he'd come to talk to her about.

Instead, he studied her over the top of his glass with a half-smile playing on his lips. His hazel eyes were half lidded and his expression difficult to read. He looked thinner and more tanned than he had a year earlier.

Cheating must agree with him.

No, she shouldn't think that way, it was all in the past and she'd forgiven him so she could move on with her life. The last thing she needed now was to dwell on past hurts and get worked up all over again. Besides, she and Athol were dating and having a wonderful time together. He treated her the way she wished Andy had throughout their marriage. That reminded her, she should call Athol before bed, see if he wanted to have dinner tomorrow night. She hadn't seen him since the previous weekend.

"Strange to be sitting here together, just the two of us," she continued.

"And yet it feels so perfectly natural," he said.

Her eyebrows arched. "Yes, we've certainly spent many an hour in this exact spot."

"Some of my happiest memories."

Cindy's eyes narrowed. What was this all about? She didn't mean to be rude, but her back was killing her, her feet ached, and all she wanted to do was lie on the couch with a glass of wine and watch the latest episode of *Better Homes and Gardens* on catch up TV. "Yes, indeed."

At her feet, Petal curled into a ball, eyes shut. Her thick white fur tickled Cindy's ankles as she moved in her sleep. Probably chasing something in her dreams. Cindy smiled down at the dog, then returned her attention to Andy.

He cleared his throat. "This looks delicious." He picked up a hot spring roll, dipped it in sweet chilli sauce, and took a bite.

"Just a bit of this and that." Cindy reached for a dumpling and popped it into her mouth.

He swallowed. "I wanted to come over and have a chat, just you and me. Like we used to, remember?"

"Of course I remember, I'm not senile," she retorted.

He laughed. "Sorry, I know you're not."

"What's on your mind, Andy? You seem anxious, which is very unlike you and is making me a bit uncomfortable."

He shook his head. "You know me so well."

She sniffed. "Well, we grew up together and then we were married for almost forty years. So yes, I'd say I know pretty much everything there is to know about you." She'd always been able to read him like a book. Apart from the fact that he'd cheated on her for years. She hadn't known that little tidbit of information about him until he walked out on her. But now wasn't the time to raise the subject again. What she really wanted was for him to leave so she could put her feet up, and instigating an argument about what had or had not happened, and whose fault it was, was the least likely way to achieve that goal.

"That's what I wanted to talk to you about."

"How well we know one another?" Cindy's internal alarm bell rang. Nerves jittered.

Andy leaned forward, reached across the table to take her hand in his. She'd missed that simple gesture so much in recent years. Not only since he'd left, but for the years before it when he'd paid her less and less attention.

"You and me, we have a history together," he began, his gaze earnest. "We shouldn't throw that away so easily. I know it was my fault, that I was the one to give up, but now I'm beginning to see how much of a mistake that was."

The words coming from his mouth were exactly what Cindy had hoped to hear a year earlier. In fact, he'd taken her for granted for a long time. She'd wished for him to come to the realisation of what she meant to him any number of times in the past decade. But now?

"Andy, we're divorced."

"I know, but that's a technicality. Nothing more. In our hearts we're still joined. I know you feel that as much as I do. I want us to give it another go, take another chance on each other. What do you think?"

* * *

BEN

The wind rushed over Ben's bike helmet as he pedalled. He blinked, his eyes dry from the hot air. What would he say? He still hadn't exactly got his thoughts lined up in a coherent way as he usually would. He rarely let his emotions take over, but it seemed today that'd be difficult to manage.

He was angry. Hurt as well.

No matter how many times he'd run through the scenario in his head since that swim in the ocean when he'd first begun chipping away at the resolve to move on with his life and leave the past where it lay, he couldn't let it go.

Why had Diana given him up? Why had she never told Andy about him? Did she know how much that'd robbed him of the chance to grow up understanding who he was?

He didn't regret his childhood; far from it. Wouldn't swap his parents for anyone or anything. Still, he could've known Diana and Andy — had some kind of relationship with them. That would've been enough, perhaps. It might've helped him feel grounded in the knowledge of who he was, where he'd come from. It could've helped him overcome the painful shyness he'd been tormented by as a boy.

Diana's house was a small, brick structure in a retirement community. The smooth streets were lined with manicured garden beds and perfectly trimmed shrubbery. He pulled the bike up onto the curb and rested it against the attached single car garage. The helmet came off easily but left his hair a sweaty mess which he scrubbed quickly with both hands as if that might somehow make him more presentable. He set it on the handlebars and strode to the front door.

A loud knock brought Diana to the door. Her eyes lit up and she offered him a hug before ushering him into the living room.

"I'm so glad you stopped by," she said. "Can I get you a drink — tea, coffee, water?"

"Water would be great, thanks."

She disappeared through an archway and soon returned with two tall glasses of cold water and handed him one, then they both sat across from each other on matching couches.

"You rode your bike here, I see."

He nodded. "I like riding around the Cove. It doesn't take long to get anywhere. I hardly use my car these days."

"Very good exercise too," she agreed with a wide smile. "You're so fit, you look as though you could run one of those marathons."

He grunted. "I've run a half-marathon before. Maybe I'll do another one. It's something to consider, anyway. I don't exactly have a full-schedule."

"Is everything okay, Ben?" her smile faded at his tone.

He tapped out a silent rhythm on the arm of the

couch with his fingertips. "I'm fine. Only, I've been thinking about something and I wanted to ask you a question."

She quirked an eyebrow. "Okay."

His gaze locked on hers. He had her eyes. His same dark brown gaze staring back at him tripped him up, making him pause and blink.

"Um, well, it's about us — you and me. When you found out you were pregnant, I suppose I'd like to know what you were thinking. You had nine months, or almost that, to figure things out. During that time, didn't you once think that maybe you could raise me? Or that you should tell Andy about me?"

Diana leaned back in her chair with a sigh. "I did think those things. But I was so young, and my parents soon convinced me otherwise. They told me I couldn't do it, that they wouldn't help me — how would I make it on my own as a teenager with a child to feed? They were right of course, you are as well. There's no easy answer, but to be honest with you as much pain as all of this has caused me throughout my life, my one consolation is knowing you were raised by two wonderful, loving parents."

He tipped forward, leaned his elbows on his knees, hands fidgeting with one another. "Yes, I understand that — and I'm happy I was raised by them as well. But I'd like to know why you never told Andy. I get that you needed to sever contact with me, that was your choice — but he didn't have a choice. You took that away from him. He may have wanted to be in my life. Did you ever think of that?"

"Of course." Her lower lip trembled, and she bit down on it.

He waited, anger pulsating through his veins. It

made no sense for him to be angry at this sweet old lady who just happened to be his birth mother. She watched him through glistening eyes, eyes so much like his own. He didn't want to hurt her, hadn't intended to when he rode through town to see her. But it was almost as though he couldn't help himself — emotions he'd repressed his whole life leapt to the surface, making his heart ache and his throat throb with the intensity of it all.

"Of course you thought about it? But what happened — why didn't you *do* anything about it?"

"Things were different back then. Young girls didn't have babies in high school. They just didn't. I was a good girl, at least until that night I was. The apple of my father's eye. He looked at me differently after I told him I was pregnant; it broke me in a way I hadn't expected. I gave in to them after that, anything they wanted. I went along with it because of the way my father had looked at me. I didn't want to be the girl he so clearly saw; I wanted to earn back his love. And I did. As soon as you were gone, he pretended none of it'd happened at all and went back to being the doting father he'd been. Of course, we both knew nothing would ever quite be the same. I'd done what he wanted, and he gave back the love he'd taken away — but at a great cost that I didn't fully understand at the time. Not until much later, when Rupert and I discovered we weren't able to have children."

Ben had thought hearing her explanation of things would help him achieve some kind of closure, some inner peace that would descend over him and help him be able to better accept his life the way it was. But it didn't work. Her words only incensed him further. She was speaking about him as though he were an obstacle in the way of her happiness that had to be removed, not a baby — her child.

He stood to his feet and paced to one side of the room, the tremor in his voice betraying the intensity of his emotions. "After I was sent away, everyone got what they wanted: your father got to pretend I didn't exist, you won back his love, and everyone lived happily ever after — except for one thing! I was a baby, a child without a mother or father to love me until my adoptive parents came along! Did you even consider that I might end up in the system for years with no one to love me? Did you think about me at all?"

Diana gaped. "Of course I did. I've told you that over and over. I couldn't stop thinking about you. I'm sorry about everything. Really, I am. I should've told Andy about you — but it was a complicated situation. What should I have said? I mean, he was in a serious relationship with my best friend. I'd have lost her and my parents — everyone in my life. I was so young" She reached for him, grasped his arm with her hand, her eyes begging.

He inhaled a deep breath, willing his anger to dissipate, his heart rate to slow. He patted her hand. "I understand."

When he walked away, he muttered beneath his breath. "But I can't forgive you."

CHAPTER 23

FRANKLIN

*W*ith a whir, the photocopier puffed to a halt. Franklin waited, eyes narrowed. What was going on? A beep, then nothing. He slapped the side of the machine with his open palm and studied the control panel.

The words 'paper jam' blinked back at him, along with a complicated map of some kind he supposed indicated where the jam could be located.

Great. Just what he needed.

With a grunt, he let his finger trail over the map. There was a panel at the end that should open. He leaned over, tugged it, and the panel responded. Now what?

The next thing to do was open a side door, but where was it? No amount of tugging shifted anything and he shook his head, frustration mounting.

This was ridiculous.

He studied the map again, this time finding the door it indicated, and pulling it open. Another grunt, this time in victory. If only Rebecca were here, she'd have the jam sorted out in no time.

Nerves jangled in his stomach when thoughts of Rebecca flashed through his mind. She was due to return to the Cove from Sydney today. She'd flown down south to spend time with her family, and he hadn't seen her in the almost two weeks since their shared kiss.

He found the wayward sheet of paper and extracted it from the machine. Smiling in triumph, he closed the panels and doors and pressed the button again. This time it whirred to life and spat out the copies he needed at one end.

They hadn't spoken about the kiss yet. It wasn't something he wanted to discuss over the phone. Besides, he was always awkward on the phone; there was something disconcerting about speaking to a person you had shared such an intimate moment with without seeing them face-to-face. Still, he itched to find out what she was thinking about the whole thing.

Steph had suggested he do one of those video calls, but that seemed as though it'd be even more awkward. He was horrible at selfies. He had attempted a few with the surf behind him when the waves were particularly good, and they always ended up showing a brilliant view of his nostril hairs, but the surf - not so much. He wasn't the selfie kind of guy, so a video call angled up his nose wasn't exactly the way he wanted to discuss something as monumental as the kiss that'd changed everything between them. The kiss he hadn't been able to stop thinking about since.

There was more to it than that, of course. The

additional complicating factor was, he was her boss. He'd stepped over the line. It was inappropriate - or romantic. There was no way of knowing which train of thought she was on — but one could be devastating, the other life-changing.

No, this was a conversation they needed to have in person. That way there was less chance of any misunderstandings.

To his way of thinking, the kiss had been a long time coming. But as far as he knew, Bec might be wondering how to break the news to him that the kiss wasn't as good for her as it was him, or even worse, that it was inappropriate and unprofessional. Which, of course, it was.

Ugh.

He gathered the sheaf of papers to his chest. The waiting was the worst. Not knowing was killing him. He could go back and forth about it all day long in his head, but what he really needed to do was to have a private conversation with Bec.

A noise caught his ear. He glanced up as the office door opened, and Bec stepped through, wearing her freshly pressed navy police uniform, and her brown hair pulled back into a tight ponytail at the nape of her neck. Deep brown eyes flitted up to meet his as a spark of electricity crashed through his body. This was ridiculous. He wasn't a teenager anymore. So why was his body responding as though he was one?

He was a grown man, in charge of this police station and responsible for policing all of Emerald Cove. He could handle a little crush. If Bec didn't want to take things between them any further, he could swallow his own feelings and continue to work with her in a professional manner.

She smiled, her eyes crinkling at the corners.

Oh crud.

He offered her a half-hearted smile. His nerves got the better of him. He shuffled the papers against his chest and cleared his throat, acutely aware of her progress across the office towards him.

"Hi boss," she said.

He faced her with a wide grin. What he really wanted to do was wrap her in his arms and kiss her with every ounce of passion welling up inside him. But that would be completely inappropriate given they were both standing in the office — even if no one else was paying any attention to them at that moment. Instead, he cleared his throat with a grunt.

"Hey, Proby. Good to see you. How was Sydney?"

She smiled, her cheeks pink. "Sydney was nice. It was so good to go home, even if it was only for a little while. I got to see everyone, relax with the family — it's been a long time."

Her eyes glistened, lips pursed.

"Are you okay?" He took a step towards her.

"I'm fine. Thanks, and you? I wish I didn't have to leave so soon after the funeral. If I hadn't had a flight already booked…"

He shook his head. "No, you couldn't miss that flight. You needed to go home and see everyone after everything you've been through. I've been coping okay. I have enough casseroles, pies, and slices in the fridge to feed an army for the next decade. I'm being well taken care of."

She grinned. "Well, that's good to hear. At least you know how much the community loves you."

He grunted. "If food is love, then apparently I'm adored."

She laughed. "If you need help eating it, let me know."

Was that an opening or was he imagining things? "That would be great. I can bring you a casserole if you like?"

"Okay."

"Or you could come over and share one with me," he offered, cheeks flaming.

"Perfect. I'd love that."

They stared at each other for a few long moments, both smiling. His heart thundered against his ribcage.

"Uh, I suppose…"

"Yeah, I'd better get some work done," she finished, her face a little more flushed than usual.

"Excuse me, boss! I don't mean to interrupt but I haven't been able to reach you on your desk phone." Steph poked her head through the open office doorway, red curls askew in a messy bun. "Ethan Flannigan's been trying to call you. He says it's important."

"Okay, thanks. Tell him I'll be right there."

He combed his fingers through his hair and faced Rebecca. "We'll talk later?"

"Yeah, sure. We'll talk later," she replied.

As he walked back to his office a smile slid over his lips. She'd agreed to come over for a meal — surely that was a good sign.

He sat at his desk and picked up the phone, which was lit up like a Christmas tree. Every line blinked green. He frowned. Something was going on.

"Hello? This is Sergeant Franklin. Can I help you?"

"Sarge, hold on a minute. Just turning up the TV."

"Is that you, Ethan?"

"Yeah. Hey, Sarge. Listen, have you been watching the weather station?" Ethan Flannigan was a friend who'd moved back to the Cove to run the Seaside Manor Bed and Breakfast. They'd grown up together although Ethan was a little younger than Franklin. They'd always gotten along well. Each loved surfing, skate boarding, and the outdoors as much as the other.

"Uh, no. Not since breakfast. I've been dealing with a, ahem, photocopier situation."

"Ah, okay then. Well, it looks like the cyclone that's been headed southwest from Bowen — Zelda, they're calling it — has gotten stronger and is aiming right for the Cove, according to the weather forecasters on Channel Seven."

"Hmmm. I've been keeping an eye on that one. It must've shifted course," replied Franklin as he sat at his desk. He clicked a browser open on his computer and navigated to the Bureau of Meteorology webpage.

"Right, I see it. Thanks for the update. Ethan. I'll take a look at it."

"No worries, Sarge. Let me know if you need any help. I'm here at the Manor doing some repairs but nothing I can't be pulled away from," replied Ethan before he hung up the phone.

Franklin studied the news headlines and noted that the weather had worsened dramatically since he watched the news earlier that morning while eating his eggs. After breakfast, he'd left for a bike ride then headed to work at the station, so he hadn't checked for an update in hours.

It wasn't unusual to get storms at this time of year, but large cyclones usually hit Northern Queensland, drove south for a bit, and petered out. They didn't often get as far south as Emerald Cove, other than with a week or so of wind and rain. This looked like it could be something more. He'd have to make certain the town was prepared.

* * *

FRANKLIN STOOD outside the station and stared up at the sky, hands pressed to his hips. Black clouds hung low, moving fast in a southerly direction. The wind buffeted him where he stood. It was humid, hot even, but with a hint of cold in the gusts of wind harrying the town.

A bolt of lightning struck at the ground in the distance, then another, followed by a faint rumble. He shook his head. They'd weathered plenty of bad storms in the Cove before, and the townsfolk knew exactly what to do. It was time to get rolling in preparation for what was to come.

Behind him footsteps echoed across the pavement.

"Something wrong, boss?" asked Rebecca.

He faced her, scratching his chin. The wind whipped her ponytail around her face. She lifted a hand to push it behind her ear.

"The cyclone's headed this way," he said. "It's up to us to make sure the community is ready for it."

"Do we have a plan?"

He nodded. "We work closely with the State Emergency Service. We've been through it plenty of times before, everyone knows what needs to get done. It's just a matter of putting the plan into action."

"Good to know."

He eyed the angry sky again. "Let's go."

Franklin gathered the team together and called in the entire staff — night shift crew, coast guard officers, water police, SES volunteers, and a representative from the Tweed Heads ambulance and fire services.

People stood or sat around the conference room, wherever they could find a space. The room was packed. Franklin pointed to the widescreen monitor mounted on the end wall where he'd displayed a map of Emerald Cove.

"The storm surge has already begun," he began. "We expect the houses along the beach will receive a battering. They've been dealing with erosion in their backyards for a decade. This might be the end of the road for some of those homes if they don't get things shored up in time. I want someone to call each and every residence and talk to them about sandbagging — most of them are prepared and familiar with what needs doing. We can help out the others — newer residents and renters."

"I'll be happy to do that," Bec raised a hand, then made a note on a pad in her lap.

He gave her a quick nod, then continued. "In a bit of bad luck, we're expecting a king tide as well."

The members of the coast guard groaned as one.

"Never mind. We've dealt with this kind of thing before, and we will again, no doubt," he continued. "We need to make sure everyone's prepared. Coast Guard team — you can go up and down the shore and tell everyone who's fishing off the rocks, or out in small boats in the Cove, that it's time to pack up and go home."

The team nodded, murmuring amongst themselves.

Franklin waited for quiet. "We also need to put in a call to the surf lifesavers to close the beaches."

"I'll do that, since I'm going to be on the phone anyway," offered Bec.

"Thank you, Bec," he replied, aware all of a sudden that he'd used her first name in front of the group, instead of the usual term of endearment for all first year, probationary officers. He'd called her Proby whenever they were in the office, since she'd arrived. He hoped no one else had noticed.

Words caught in his throat. It was hot in the conference room, more so than usual with so many people standing shoulder-to-shoulder or crowded around the long conference table.

Steph raised a hand. He offered her a quick nod to give her the floor.

"I've put in a call to the shelters," she said. "They're already preparing bedding, food, and water in case people have to evacuate their homes."

"That's good news," replied Franklin. "Thank you, Steph."

People moved restlessly around the room. Muttered conversation broke out.

Franklin waved both hands. "Okay. All right. I know you're keen to get moving, so I won't keep you any longer. Let's stay in touch via the radio. I think everyone has their duties to perform. The rest of us will work to ensure all members of the community are safe and sound, tucked away in their homes. I'll call the local media and get them to put out a notice to the community to tie down anything in the yard that could become a hazard if picked up by the wind. No doubt they'll want me to make some kind of statement." He shook his head. "So, I guess that one's up to me." He had no time for the media usually; they did nothing but get in his way or spread fear in his opinion. But there were times they came in handy, and this was one of them. So, he'd have to put a tie around his neck, brush his hair, and plaster a smile on his face.

"Better get dolled up for the camera, boss," called one of the coast guard. "Put some gel in your hair."

Everyone laughed.

Franklin dismissed the meeting and the team went about doing the tasks that had been assigned to them. He stayed behind to wipe down the whiteboard where they'd written some strategy notes earlier in the meeting.

Bec appeared at his side. "Do you need my help with anything else?" she asked.

He crossed his arms over his chest, doing his best to subdue the feelings surging within. "Ah, no, I think that's all. Just keep yourself safe," he said. "And check in with me every now and then."

"Will do, boss," she replied with a smile.

He watched her saunter from the room and wondered how on earth he was going to be able to do his job feeling the way he did. It was highly distracting. Which frustrated him more than anything else — he'd had his fair share of relationship disasters and personal issues over the years. But none had ever impacted his job performance. He'd prided himself on doing his job well, putting the community first. But now, he felt scattered, as though he couldn't keep his mind fixed on the task at hand. With a shake of the head he returned his attention to the whiteboard. He'd known since the first moment she walked into his office that she'd likely be the death of him, but he'd underestimated how.

CHAPTER 24

REBECCA

$\mathcal{T}$he Emerald Cove Community Centre was nestled between two large brick buildings, one for the volunteer fire department and the other for the Commonwealth Bank.

From the outside it looked like a simple single-story structure with weathered red bricks and cracked white paint on the trim. However, underneath the basketball courts and meeting rooms, soup kitchen, and gym, was a full basement used by the community for a variety of things which included the provision of temporary accommodation during storms or other emergencies.

Rebecca helped the volunteers pull thin plastic-covered mattresses from the storage cupboards and haul them over to line up along the floor. Then, puffing hard she sat on one of the many folding chairs scattered around the outside of the basement to catch her breath.

They'd already set up a food and drinks table, a first aid table, and some craft activities on a third table for any children who might show up. With the mattresses and sleeping bags in place, the only thing left to do was to make sure the volunteer staff who'd be manning the place were on top of the procedures to follow for checking in members of the community to make sure everyone was accounted for and treated for injuries before they settled in.

It was possible they wouldn't need it at all, and the cyclone would change course and swing out to sea, missing the Cove entirely, but they should be prepared just in case. It was the first time she'd had to run through the storm preparedness protocol. She was grateful for the help from the State Emergency Services volunteers who'd done it all plenty of times before and had patiently explained everything that needed doing.

"I think we can take it from here, Constable, if you've got other things you need to do," said Diana Jones, one of the SES volunteers. Her brown bob slipped forward as she knelt beside a mattress and carefully smoothed a sleeping bag in place on top of it. She'd always been kind to Rebecca, one of the few people who'd checked in on her at the hospital when she was injured.

"Thanks Diana, I think I'll head out and check on some of the local businesses, make sure they're prepared. You've got my number if you need anything, or you can call the switchboard and they'll radio me."

Diana nodded and struggled to her feet with a grunt. "You've got it."

* * *

THE REST of Rebecca's afternoon was spent driving around town, helping business owners secure their businesses for the rising storm. Rain pummelled the town and gutters had already overflowed, pouring storm water onto the streets. Drains roared with water, and the wind slammed her car in gusts that pushed it sideways when she wasn't expecting it, making her heart jitter in her chest.

As Rebecca cruised by the beach for the tenth time in less than an hour, she noticed the waves were lashing the jetty much higher up and wilder than the usual gentle rolling peaks that lapped against the pylons. Foam drifted up the beach on the king tide. Each wave seemed to draw closer to the sand dunes and the fence that separated the parklands from the dunes.

She swallowed and shook her head as adrenaline pumped through her veins. The storm had arrived and so far it was every bit as ominous as the weather forecasters had promised it would be.

Fat raindrops splattered against her windscreen and she turned up the wipers until they were whizzing back and forth at high speed. She slowed her pace, unable to see more than a few metres ahead.

So far, she'd managed to visit most businesses in the area, and everyone was as prepared to weather the storm as they could be. Some business owners had chosen to close up shop and go home, while others, like Foodstore were still open in case anyone needed supplies.

"And besides," Marg had said, her blue hair frizzing about her head in wild curls, "we've weathered enough storms to know we'll get through this one just fine as well."

The cruiser dipped to one side as she came too near to the curb. Rebecca corrected, but not before sending a wave of storm water across the footpath. Thankfully, there was no one around, and even if there had been, they could hardly get more wet if they were out walking in *this* weather.

She shook her head, her gaze flitting from one side of the street to the other, double-checking that everything loose had been secured, every window closed, every shop front sand-bagged. There was no telling how high the tide would get, but it wasn't likely to make it onto the street. Still, they liked to be prepared for every eventuality — just in case.

A flash of blue caught her eye through the haze of rain. What was that? Someone was walking slowly along the footpath. They turned onto the pedestrian crossing right in front of Rebecca, then stumbled and fell.

She hit the brakes then climbed out and hurried to help. An elderly woman lay on the road, one hand braced on the tarmac in front of her, both legs tucked up as though to bring some kind of comfort.

"Are you okay?" called Rebecca, above the noise of the storm.

Thunder growled nearby and the sky lit up with a flash, followed by a loud boom. Rainwater blinded her. She held up a hand above the brim of her hat to protect her vision.

The woman glanced up at her. "Oh hello, officer. Do you think you could help me up?"

* * *

THE WOMAN'S name was Rose. She didn't remember anything else about herself. There was a little scrape on both knees but otherwise paramedics hadn't found anything wrong with her and had said she could go home.

But that's exactly where the problem began.

They sat side by side on the tailgate of the ambulance Rebecca had called as soon as she found Rose.

"So, you're not sure where you live?" asked Rebecca.

The woman peered through narrowed eyes out at the torrential rain soaking the small town of Emerald Cove.

"Um let me see. It might be down that way," she pointed in the direction of the main beach. "Or perhaps the other way."

"Can you please check your pockets for me?" asked Rebecca. "Maybe you have some ID on you."

The woman patted all of her pockets and found tissues in one, a lip balm in another, and nothing more. She hadn't been carrying a purse when Rebecca found her sprawled on the road.

So, what now?

"We've got other calls coming in, so we have to go," said Steve, one of the paramedics.

Rebecca and Rose stood up. Steve shut the back doors, waved goodbye and he and his partner drove off into the storm. Rebecca took off her hat and rubbed a hand over her soaked hair. She replaced the hat with a sigh.

"Well come on, Rose. We can't stay out in this weather. I'll take you to the evacuation centre for now. They have showers, clothes you can change into, and warm blankets."

"Hot chocolate?" asked Rose, her red-rimmed eyes hopeful.

"The best hot chocolate around," replied Rebecca with a grin.

She helped Rose into the cruiser, then drove her down to the Community Centre. Diana found Rose some clothes and took her to the showers.

Rebecca waved goodbye, called out that she'd check on her later, and spun on her heel to leave. Then she spotted Franklin on the other side of the room talking to a group.

His eyes met hers at the same time and he nodded in her direction, returning his attention to the people around him. She hesitated. Should she say something or leave him to it? He was her boss, after all, and they'd only communicated by radio for most of the day. She'd never felt awkward about talking to him before. On any normal day she'd stride over to him and join the conversation.

She squared her shoulders. It would be strange for her to leave; he'd think something was wrong. Which it most definitely wasn't. Not wrong exactly, simply awkward, strange and about a thousand other things that basically meant now whenever she saw him her heart leapt and her stomach lurched all at the same time.

Kissing him had changed things between them. It was everything she'd been wanting. She only hoped he felt the same way.

She moved towards him just as he finished up his conversation and headed her way. They met in the middle — he almost ran into her, hadn't noticed her walking towards him. He grunted, laughed, patted her on the shoulder in a strange, red-cheeked move that made her shake her head.

"There you are. How's it going?"

Something about standing so close to him made words catch in her throat. She coughed. "I brought in an older woman, Rose. Doesn't seem to remember anything about her life — no last name, no purse or ID. So, she's with Diana who's promised to care for her until I can get something sorted. I thought I'd call the aged care facilities in the area, see if anyone's missing."

"Good, sounds like you've got it under control." Franklin pressed his hands to his hips, brown eyes sparkling as they met her gaze.

She smiled. "You okay?"

He nodded. "Fine. Everyone seems to be set, we've already got a few evacuees staying here."

"I saw that."

"The roof was blown off two houses so far that we know of. SES is out there, doing what they can to cover the holes with tarps."

"I'm sure there'll be more roofs to go. That wind is getting vicious," she replied.

Silence descended between them. On the other side of the room people called to each other and laughed. Someone threw a handball against the wall, where it bounced on the floor, back to the wall, hit the floor again. Over and over.

Rebecca pushed her hands deep into her pockets, chewed the inside of her cheek. "I have to get going."

"Yeah me too. We should catch up later."

She smiled. "Sounds good."

As she walked away, she rolled her eyes, her face flaming. Well, that wasn't awkward at all.

CHAPTER 25

CINDY

*H*er mind wasn't on what she was doing. Cindy drove down the main street and straight past Foodstore. Where was she going again? Oh, that's right — she needed to stock up on groceries. The storm had grown worse and who knew how long she'd be stuck at home. She needed toilet paper, milk, and bread. And she had to hurry, or she'd be blown away entirely the way the wind was picking up.

The funny thing was, living alone, she rarely ate bread anymore. She generally kept a loaf in the freezer and ate one slice at a time, hot from the toaster. But otherwise, she didn't consume it the way she had in the past - no sandwiches for her anymore. If she left it on the bench it grew mouldy long before she managed to use it up, so she'd shifted to eating other things for lunch — crackers with cheese, olives and smoked salmon, or crispbread with avocado and tuna.

She spun the car around at the next opportunity for a U-turn and headed back to the shops.

Focusing on what she was doing had become impossible ever since Andy's visit to her house the other night. Even that thought was a strange one, since for decades it'd been *their* house, and now it was *hers*. But his bombshell had taken her completely by surprise. There were many things she expected to hear come from her ex-husband's mouth, but wanting her back was the last thing she thought she'd ever hear him say.

Cindy pulled the car into the parking lot, dodging puddles that looked as though they might swallow her and the vehicle whole. She found a spot as close to the shop front as she could, tugged on her raincoat, and climbed out of the car, wrestling with the fabric bags she'd pushed onto her arm once they caught in the wind.

"Ugh, come here, you ridiculous — ouch!" One of the bags tightened around her arm and she hopped in place to keep from tripping on the others that fell to the ground at her feet. Then she scooped them up and kept moving, bending her head into the howling wind.

When the automatic door swished shut behind her, she breathed a sigh of relief.

"Looks like it's getting pretty bad out there!" called Marg from the deli counter at the back of the shop, when she saw Cindy making her way down the bakery aisle.

Cindy nodded and reached for a loaf of bread. "It's as bad as I've ever seen. No hail yet, so that's a blessing."

"True enough. We haven't seen a soul in here for the last hour. Boss says we're closing up and heading home in five minutes. You should get to shelter as well."

Cindy waved a hand in Marg's direction. "Will do, honey. You stay safe now, okay?"

Marg blew her a kiss. Smiling, Cindy grabbed the other things she needed and made her way to the register. The staff were putting things away, locking doors, and shutting off lights even as they checked her out. She hurried to put her bags away in the car, the rain and wind battering her as she scurried.

When she pulled out of the parking lot, she let the car idle a few moments as she peered down the road. The cafe was still open by the looks of it. She'd asked Crystal to shut up and go home, but she could see lights on and cars in the parking spaces beside the building.

With a shake of the head, she pulled out onto the road and headed for the cafe. It was only a little way down the road, almost directly across the street from Foodstore. Still, she had to manoeuvre across a median strip — thankfully, no police around that she could see, or otherwise she'd have had to go all the way to the end of the street, around the roundabout and back again.

The noise of the rain on the roof and windows was deafening. She parked beside the cafe, pulled her sodden raincoat back on, and scurried as fast as she could manage without slipping and sliding on the wet pavement in through the front door.

The entire cafe was lit up. A few guests still huddled in one corner of the room. Crystal strode to greet her immediately.

"Hey Cindy, I didn't think you were coming."

Cindy's brow furrowed. "Why are there still customers in the restaurant?"

Crystal shrugged. "They won't leave." Her long black hair brushed her hips, straight and sleek with a streak of pink down one side. A black apron was tied neatly around her thin waist, covering a paisley printed top and black mini skirt.

Cindy offered her a smile laced with irritation. "Then you make them leave, Crystal. Come on, let's get on with it then. We've got to get this place closed up or the SES will be on our case in no time. Besides, I want you home safe and sound. We don't know if things will get worse, but just in case…"

Crystal nodded. "Okay."

"So?" Cindy motioned towards the customers.

"I don't want to do it. Can't you?"

"You've got to learn to deal with confrontation some time, Crissie."

Crystal chewed on her fingernails, one arm resting protectively across her middle. "I know, one day."

With a roll of the eyes Cindy marched over to the table full of customers. They'd finished their coffees. Plates littered with half eaten desserts were strewn around the table. They were laughing at something one of the women had said when she arrived, and looked up, the group growing suddenly quiet at the expression on Cindy's face.

"Hello folks. Just letting you know we're closing the cafe."

"Give us another half hour, love," replied one of the men with a wink.

Cindy's blood boiled. She shook her head. "Sorry sir, we're closing now. So, you'll have to leave right this very moment. There's a cyclone if you haven't noticed."

"Just a storm, it'll blow over," continued the man.

"Time's up," she replied, pressing her hands to her hips and fixing her gaze on his.

They made their apologies and wandered in dribs and drabs from the restaurant muttering about how they'd get wet, and didn't the cafe have any umbrellas they could borrow?

She usually would've given them umbrellas from the cafe's stash, but after their attitudes she didn't have any desire to help them further. They'd clearly been ignoring Crystal for at least an hour since that's when Cindy had called and asked her to close up. So, if they never came back again, as far as she was concerned it was good riddance.

"That was amazing," whispered Crystal as she trotted alongside Cindy to the front door where Cindy locked up and switched out the lights.

Cindy grinned. "One day I'd love to see you do it too. Now let's get those dishes cleared so we can go home."

WITH A HAND WAVING over her head, Cindy watched as Crystal and the kitchen staff pulled carefully out of the parking lot to head home. Now the wind was higher still, and debris tumbled along the street. One glance at the beach revealed foam higher on the sand than she was tall, and enormous waves crashing to shore.

Tugging her raincoat tighter around her body, she muttered a prayer, and bent forwards to push through the wind and rain to her car.

She should be at home tucked up on the couch with a blanket over her knees and a cup of tea on the side table, watching a romantic comedy or reading the latest mystery. This was the last place she wanted to be.

She'd never intended to be out in the storm so late. She was very much regretting not coming directly to the cafe to close it up herself although Crystal had assured her she could take care of it, and Cindy was doing her best to release some of the responsibility for managing the place to her staff. Moments like this were when it seemed perfectly clear to her that time may never come.

The car was locked, which she must've done as a reflex. Her hands were slippery, and she couldn't seem to get the button to work in unlocking it. A large beach umbrella tumbled by along the road in front of the cafe. It turned, end over end, moving fast. She watched it, her brow furrowed. It was far too heavy for her to lift and moving too quickly for her to catch.

Her eyes widened when she saw a woman step out of Foodstore with a bag over her arm and onto the road without looking up. It was Keisha. She would recognise that haughty head toss anywhere, and the designer rain jacket in red with a fur style trim stood out like a sore thumb in Emerald Cove.

"Keisha look out!" shouted Cindy.

Her voice didn't carry on the wind, instead it was whisked away from her mouth and muffled by the crash of thunder.

She watched in horror, unable to move, as the umbrella hurtled down the road and slammed directly into Keisha, sending her flying. Her shopping bag dropped to the road and fruit rolled out. Keisha landed on her back and didn't move as the umbrella hesitated a moment, then continued on its way.

Cindy set off at a trot, the best she could manage in the conditions, her arms helicoptering at her sides to keep her balance.

By the time she reached Keisha, she was puffing hard. She really should look into getting a treadmill for the house, or perhaps join the local aerobics class at the gym. Her exercise routine usually involved a stroll on the beach and some gardening. But after working all day at the cafe, she didn't have the energy for more than that most days.

She bent down beside Keisha, patted her shoulder.

"Keisha, honey, wake up!"

Keisha's eyes were closed, but flitted open at the sound of Cindy's voice. She groaned and reached up a hand to press to her head.

"Keisha, can you stand up? You're in the middle of the road, honey, and the visibility out here is terrible. We've got to get you off this road if you can move."

Keisha blinked a few times, then struggled to her feet with Cindy's help. Cindy held an arm beneath Keisha's, doing her best to support the other woman's weight.

They began the arduous process of hobbling to the footpath. Keisha cried out with pain and pressed a hand to her side with each step.

"That's it, you're doing great. When we get to the footpath you can sit, and I'll call an ambulance. Keep going."

There was a shout behind them, almost drowned out by the noise of the storm. Cindy glanced back over her shoulder and saw Andy standing at the top of the stairs just outside Foodstore's glass doors. His face was pale with panic, one arm outstretched, pointing.

Her gaze followed the direction he was pointing, and she saw it — a delivery truck headed their way.

Adrenaline jolted Cindy into action. "Okay honey, we've got to move faster. Come on!"

She propelled Keisha forward with every ounce of strength she could muster. They stepped up onto the curb as the truck whooshed by behind them, the water from its tyres washing over them in a great, muddy wave that soaked the back of Cindy's jeans and filled her shoes with even more water than they already contained. She stumbled, landing on her knees with a grunt. Falling forward onto her hands, she felt them skid along the pavement. Her heart thundered against her ribcage and adrenaline made her head light.

Keisha reached the wall of the cafe and leaned against it. Cindy stood slowly, already feeling the pain in her knees tightening her legs. A quick study of her palms found them red and grazed.

"Well done, Keisha. Now, let's get you inside and call the ambulance to come and check you out." She hobbled over to Keisha's side.

Andy reached them then, his eyes wide and the brim of his sun hat sagging under the weight of water. "You were almost killed!" he cried. "What on earth?"

"Keisha's hurt," replied Cindy. "Let's get her inside and I'll tell you all about it."

* * *

REBECCA

The hospital was quiet. It wasn't that they didn't have plenty of patients to care for, but after the noise outside — the buffeting wind, the bucketing rain, the crack of thunder, the howl of sirens — Rebecca embraced the relative peace and calm of the hospital's emergency waiting room.

She'd responded to a call for an ambulance at the Emerald Cafe to bring Keisha Pham to the hospital. Since she was close by, she thought she'd attend as well and check out what'd happened. When she arrived at the cafe, the ambulance was only minutes out and she'd found Cindy, Andy, and Keisha there, with Keisha laid out on the carpeted floor of the entry way, a cold compress on her forehead.

Cindy and Andy were on the other side of the room having a heated conversation in whispers she couldn't understand. She cleared her throat to announce her presence and they hurried to greet her with wide smiles.

That had to be an awkward situation. She hoped having her there made it a little easier on them. But regardless, it wasn't long before the ambulance arrived. Keisha left with the paramedics, Andy followed in his car, and Rebecca trailed after them. She wasn't needed but with the weather conditions thought it made sense to keep an eye on the ambulance as it made its way to the hospital.

Now that she was here, there wasn't much she could do. She might as well head back to the station. Her shift was over, but perhaps they'd need her to help with something there or at the evacuation centre. Besides, she'd barely had a thing to eat or drink all day long. She could use a coffee and a muffin or whatever she could find in the kitchen at the station.

The drive back to the station was a nail-biter as the wind buffeted the cruiser from the left and behind. The car almost fishtailed a few times, but she managed to keep it on track, driving slowly and peering over the steering wheel into the downpour with narrowed eyes.

Finally, she pulled into the car park outside the police station, and with a sigh of relief let the tension ease from her neck and shoulders. The light show and booming thunder had ended, but the rain and wind were unrelenting.

Inside the reception area she shook the water from her raincoat and peeled it from her uniform then ran her hands over her hair to smooth it back into place. Her stomach growled. The reception area was dark, so no doubt everyone was busy somewhere — Steph would've gone home to her family by this time of day, but the rest of the team were likely to be out and about rescuing stranded citizens, clearing roads, or pulling tarpaulins over broken roofs alongside the fire crews and SES volunteers.

She'd join them again just as soon as she could rustle up something to eat in the kitchen. She hung her raincoat on a hook by the door, locked it behind her, and made her way into the office.

The kitchen light was on, which was strange since the rest of the office was bathed in darkness. She peeked inside and found Franklin leaned against one of the benches, eating a lamington. Flakes of coconut clung to the corners of his mouth and his eyes were pressed shut in delight as he munched on the choco-late covered treat. They blinked open when she cleared her throat.

"Well, well, it looks like I caught you in a private moment, boss. Should I come back later?"

He chewed, swallowed. "Uh, no of course not. I was hungry."

She grinned. "Well, I can relate. I'm famished. Any more where that came from?"

He pushed a white cardboard bakery box towards her and took another bite.

"Fantastic." Her stomach clenched in anticipation. She filled a coffee cup, topped it up with milk then slid one of the enormous lamingtons onto a plate and sat at the small, white kitchen table.

She waved a hand across the table, indicating for Franklin to join her. He did, setting his own coffee mug down across from her, and wiping the remnants of coconut flakes from his face.

"You finished up helping Keisha to the hospital?" he asked.

She nodded, chewing. "I thought I'd come in and see if I'm needed anywhere else."

"We're still running around rescuing people and animals. I thought I'd grab a bite to eat while I could."

"Me too."

"Great minds," he replied with a half-smile lifting the corner of his mouth.

She nodded again, too busy eating to respond. The delicious cake almost melted in her mouth. Her fingers were covered in coconut flakes and chocolate icing. There was no dainty way to eat a lamington, but in that moment, she didn't care how unattractive it made her look, she was so hungry she'd have dived into the dessert and swum laps if she could.

Franklin's phone rang and he stood to answer it, paced across the kitchen and back again, then hung up.

"Gotta go — there's a power line down and the power company is concerned someone might get hurt since visibility is so low. I said we'd go and stand guard while they work on it."

She nodded, gulped down the last of her coffee, and wiped her shirt front as she stood. "Sure thing. I'm ready."

He smiled, hesitated, then stepped towards her, taking her hands in his, then lacing his fingers through hers.

"I haven't forgotten about that night, you know."

Her heart thudded and hands tingled at his touch. Anticipation buzzed in her gut, tinged with relief at knowing he cared.

"I'm glad to hear it."

"Seeing you like this, tired, hungry, but ready to jump to action to help people — it's very attractive. Pretty hot actually. I just thought you should know."

She grinned, closed the gap between them with a quick step. "Oh yeah?"

He nodded, his lips turning up at the corners, the edges of his eyes crinkling. Yellow flecks marked the hazel, and dark lashes blinked as she wound her arms around his neck.

"I've waited a long time for you," he whispered.

Her throat tightened and she felt her heart falling, falling... there was no one else in the world for her now. She knew that with a flash of certainty as bright as the lightning that'd lit up the town all day long.

"You have? How did you know it was me you were waiting for?"

His smile broadened into a grin. "Because that first day you walked into my office you were so small and vulnerable, but the look on your face said you'd never give up. You're the one for me, Proby. I've known it all along, I just wasn't sure what to do about it until now."

"How about you kiss me then?"

When he kissed her, she tasted coconut and chocolate on his lips. His arms wrapped around her, pulling her close. In that moment her heart knew she was home.

CHAPTER 26

FRANKLIN

*T*hey'd stood guard at the power pole while the technicians worked on fixing the downed lines for an hour. Now it was dark, and Franklin needed water.

The irony of being dehydrated while wading through storm water wasn't lost on him. But the fact remained that he and Rebecca had worked hard all day long and had run out of water hours earlier. Both had forgotten to top up while they were at the station, so he was headed back there to fill their water bottles.

He cruised down the main street, past the large tree in the middle of the median that marked the centre of town. It stood outside Foodstore, regal and tall as though standing guard. Someone had strung it with fairy lights one Christmas and the entire town had loved it so much they'd never taken down the lights since. Even in the gloaming, they glowed faint, giving the tree an eerie light.

Past the tree, he glanced at Foodstore where he saw Marg Cook fumbling with the shop door. What was she doing there? From what he understood, everyone had gone home hours ago, and the shop had been locked all afternoon. With a clenched jaw he parked in front of the shop, adjusted his jacket so the hood covered his head and climbed out. The noise of the rain on his hood drowned out any other sound, so when he called out to her, he couldn't hear her response.

He jogged up the ramp to the front door and shook his hood off when he reached shelter. Water droplets sprayed a halo around him.

"This darned lock," said Marg, jostling the key in the glass door.

"You locking up or trying to get in?"

She sighed. "Locking up. I thought I'd left the meat slicers switched on, so I came back to check."

"I was wondering what you were doing here. Everyone else went home, right?"

She nodded and stepped aside for Franklin to work on the key. He jiggled it, tugged, and pulled it free.

"Ah, thank you."

"No worries. You need me to follow you home?"

She shook her head. "No, I'll be fine. I don't have far to drive, and I'll take it slow."

"Okay," he said.

He hurried back to the car, slipping his hood onto his head. As he opened the cruiser door, a buzz filled the air, followed immediately by the loudest crack he'd ever heard, as though the earth itself was splitting in two. He ducked and covered his ears out of instinct, then watched in horror as the tree in the median strip cracked apart. One half of it peeled away with a loud crunching sound and fell directly onto Foodstore's facade. The roof gave way, caving with a boom. His stomach lurched.

"Marg!" he shouted as he took off running to where he'd last seen her.

Up the stairs, he dodged around the fallen limb, the roof still creaking and cracking as it settled into place on the ground.

"Marg, can you hear me?" Louder this time. His ears strained around the sounds of the storm, attempting to pick out the sound of her voice.

"Frankie!" she called, her voice weak.

When he rounded the end of the fallen roof, he saw her, lying on the ground. She'd been pushed forwards by the roof but landed on her face with only her legs beneath the structure, the rest of her seemed plastered to the pavement.

She raised her head a little to look for him. When she saw him, she let it fall back to the footpath with a groan.

"Don't try to move, let me have a look," he said, falling to the ground beside her.

He examined her body, which was not injured from what he could tell, then felt down her legs. They were pinned in place, but not crushed it seemed.

"I'm going to pull you out," he said with a confidence he didn't feel. He didn't have a choice. Who knew how long an ambulance or fire truck would take to arrive with the weather so bad and more call outs than they could possibly manage?

"Okay," she replied.

"It might hurt."

"I figured." She groaned..

"I have to say, you gave me a bit of a fright for a moment there," he said, doing his best to distract her while he felt around the broken structure covering her legs.

"Gave me a scare as well. If you hadn't come and helped me get that darned key out of the door, well…"

She didn't have to finish her thought. He knew what she meant — she'd have been by the door, which meant she'd have been crushed by the roof, and not just pinned underneath the edge.

"You'll have to give me a few slices of your best ham as payment," he replied as he positioned his hands beneath her armpits.

She grunted. "I'll give you the whole ham, Frankie my boy. You always were my favourite. Bet you didn't know that, huh?"

He steeled himself, then pulled as hard as he dared. Marg was free. He rolled her onto her back, the rain wetting her face as she cried in silence.

"You okay?" he asked.

She nodded wordlessly, still crying.

Franklin pulled out his radio and called for an ambulance, then picked her up and carried her across the street, one arm wrapped around his neck, in the torrential rain to the Emerald Cafe. There were no chairs outside, since everything had been secured for the cyclone, and the last few steps he took were through a large and growing puddle of muddy water, but they made it and he helped Marg to sit on a concrete bench that jutted out from one of the walls.

"Sorry it's not very comfortable, but at least we're out of the rain," he said as he sat beside her. "We'll wait here for the ambos."

"It's good enough for me," she replied.

Having caught his breath, he knelt in front of her to check her legs for injuries. They'd already swollen and turned red, and there were a few large gashes oozing blood.

"How bad is it, do you think?" she asked.

He shrugged. "I don't know, but I think you'll recover — they have good colour and don't look crushed."

"That's good. The pain's really starting to pick up pace on me though." She grimaced.

He patted her arm, seating himself beside her again. "Hold on, Marg, they'll be here soon, and with any luck they'll give you the little loopy whistle everyone seems to love."

She laughed through the tears. "Well, lucky me."

CHAPTER 27

MEG

*W*hen her eyes blinked open it was pitch black in the unit. Meg rubbed her sockets with the heel of her hand and blinked again. What had woken her? One glance at the bedside table revealed fluorescent numbers on her alarm clock — three eighteen a.m.

The storm had quieted. The wind died down. Rain fell heavily outside the unit, but thankfully, being on the ground floor meant they barely heard it on the roof. Beside her, Brad slept with a peaceful sighing breath that brushed her cheek when she turned to face him.

The dog's toenails scratched the floor as she paced back and forth. She stopped beside the bed, keened, huffed, and resumed her pacing. She hated storms — especially thunder and lightning, but really any kind of weather event had her puffing, pacing, and keening all night long. Thankfully, Meg had felt so exhausted at bedtime that she'd fallen right to sleep regardless of the noise.

A sudden pain gripped her abdomen, and she rocked forward as her muscles clenched. She grunted with the shock of it, her eyes widening.

What was that? It couldn't be labour pains, she was only seven months pregnant. Perhaps it was Braxton Hicks — her midwife had told her all about that during the breastfeeding class she'd attended at the community health centre a week ago.

The pain subsided and she relaxed back onto the bed. Her heart rate slowed back to its normal pace, but now she was awake. Was it a similar pang that'd awoken her?

She padded to the bathroom, relieved herself, then stared at herself in the mirror. Her white nightgown floated around her distended stomach and breasts in the darkness, making her ghostlike.

With one hand she smoothed back her hair, then shook her head. "Please don't do this."

It was too soon to go into labour. There must be another explanation for the pain.

Another pang gripped her, bending her double in an instant. She gripped the sink, leaning towards it, her breath stuck in her chest as she moaned through the pain.

"You okay?" came Brad's sleepy voice from the bed.

She couldn't answer. Then it passed again. "No, I think I'm in labour."

"What?" Brad's voice was laced with panic. "But it's too soon."

She heard the rustling of him positioning himself

in his chair. Then he wheeled into the bathroom, eyes wide and bleary.

"I know it's too soon, so I'm hoping there's another explanation but I just don't know. It really hurts." Tears filled her voice, her throat bloated with them.

She couldn't cry, that only made the pain worse. What had the midwife said? *Breathe through the pain.*

The next contraction came faster than before, and the pain was even more intense. She breathed deep and slow, doing her best to remember the brief training session she'd sat through on labour.

When she recovered, Brad had his hand on her arm, his eyes wide with alarm. "That seemed bad."

She nodded, still puffing.

"I'm calling the ambulance," he said, wheeling away.

She didn't have the strength or will to object. It was time to go to the hospital. If she was wrong, and the baby wasn't on her way to meet them two months early, then she'd deal with that at the hospital. She couldn't risk staying home any longer.

When Brad returned, she was in the middle of another contraction. This time she'd managed her breathing better, but the pain was worsening, and she wasn't sure how much more of it she could take. She'd always planned on getting an epidural, but things seemed to be moving along faster than she'd thought they would.

Brad waited until the colour returned to her face before speaking. "They said it'll be a while, but they'll do their best to get here as fast as they can."

"A while? What does that mean?" she asked, panic raising her voice to a high pitch.

He shrugged. "I don't know, half an hour maybe. They're really busy because of the cyclone I guess."

"You guess? You guess?" she shouted, her head spinning. "I won't last half an hour."

"What do you mean?" he asked, his brow furrowed.

She leaned harder on the sink, bowing her head as another wave of pain washed over her. "I mean this baby is coming, now!"

* * *

THE NEXT HOUR was a blur for Meg. The baby didn't come as quickly as she'd thought it would and the paramedics arrived earlier than their promised half an hour travel time. So, within fifty minutes she was at the hospital with Brad by her side.

The pain had sent her into a state of focus, where she was only vaguely aware of what was going on around her, who she was with, what was said. Instead, she shut her eyes and drowned it out, doing her best to manage the agony with her breathing and keep the baby inside until the doctor saw her.

It was too early. That's what she kept thinking about — would the baby be okay?

All she wanted was for their daughter to be healthy and happy, she'd do anything to make certain of that. The anxiety left her, the worries about the future, all of it gone — instead, she focused deep within herself.

"You okay?" asked Brad, squeezing her hand as they set her up in a bed in the delivery ward.

She nodded and pursed her lips to breathe out then in again.

Her midwife, Mandy showed up, wearing scrubs and a smile.

"Hi there, Meg and Brad, how are things?"

Meg grimaced.

"It's too early, isn't it?" replied Brad.

Mandy felt Meg's abdomen with gently probing prods. "We're about eight weeks early, that's correct."

"So, is it labour?"

Meg wanted to hit him. Only she couldn't manage it. What else would it be? There was something about him in that moment that irritated her beyond belief.

"It seems like it," replied Mandy. "I'm afraid it's too late for us to stop it, although we'll try."

"Will the baby be okay?" grunted Meg.

Mandy offered her a warm smile. "Let's hope so. There's every reason to believe everything will be fine."

They stuck wires to her skin to monitor both heart beats, gave her injections, attached a drip to try to halt contractions, prepared her for the birth, and before long, she was pushing, with Mandy coaching her along the way. The obstetrician showed up at some point, although Meg didn't remember her coming into the room.

It was overwhelming. All of it. So, Meg focused again on herself, what she was feeling, what her body was doing.

She didn't want to think about the scans and the unknown illness hanging over their heads. They were about to meet her, for the first time. How would she look — would she be healthy, sickly? Would she survive the early birth?

Questions filled Meg's mind, bringing tears to her eyes. She couldn't push any longer, and sobs wracked her body.

"What's wrong?" whispered Brad, leaning in close and squeezing her hand.

"I can't do it," she cried. "I can't do it — it's too

hard. She might be sick, really sick. She may not make it — it's not meant to happen like this, she'll be too small and sickly. What if…?"

She couldn't finish her sentence as another contraction washed through her, rendering her speechless with the pain of it.

When it passed, Brad kissed her cheek. He turned her face towards him and stared into her eyes. "Baby, whatever comes we'll face it together. Okay?"

She nodded.

"Now push, my love."

"I can't."

"Yes, you can. You have to. For our daughter."

Her eyes squeezed shut, and she pushed with everything she had. When, finally, it was over, her eyes blinked open and she watched as the doctor worked on their child.

"Is she okay?"

Brad's eyes were as filled with worry as she felt.

"Brad?"

"I don't know, but you did great, baby. I'm so proud of you."

He kissed her again. She kissed him back as tears filled her eyes.

"Go and find out, honey. Please."

He nodded and followed the doctor. She couldn't hear what they said. The doctor and Mandy had the baby on a small table, with a humidicrib beside them. Brad conversed with them for a few minutes.

Soon, Mandy and Brad came back. Mandy lowered the tiny baby onto Meg's chest.

"I'd like you to meet your daughter," she said.

Meg's heart swelled at the sight of her baby. Tears fell onto her cheeks.

"Before you ask," began Brad. "She's perfect. Right Mandy?"

The midwife nodded, smiled. "The doctor says she looks completely healthy, but we'll need to run a few more tests. I'm afraid I have to take her now and she'll stay in the humidicrib for a while until we can make sure she's strong enough to leave it."

Meg kissed her daughter's cheek, then watched through blurred vision as the doctor carried her away. Brad pulled his chair closer to the bed and reached for Meg's hand again.

"You did it," he said.

She nodded, her entire being flooding with joy. "She's so beautiful."

He grinned. "And tiny."

"I can't believe…"

"There's absolutely nothing wrong with her," interrupted Brad with a shake of the head. "They were wrong."

Meg laughed, her heart bursting with love for their new daughter. "What do you think of the name, Amari? It means miracle."

His eyes glistened. "I love it. It suits her perfectly. Our little miracle."

CHAPTER 28

BEN

*T*he phone rang out again and Ben hit the 'end' button with a grunt of frustration. He'd been attempting to reach Diana for two hours without success. The last time they spoke he'd been angry and had probably hurt her feelings. The problem was, he wasn't certain if she was avoiding his calls because of that, or if there was something wrong.

The cyclone had slowed its assault for a while but was again howling around the eaves of his house and drenching the town with bucketing rain. Ben paced to the window and peered out through the blinds at the storm. It was dark now, so hard to see any further than the fence that surrounded his home. Rain blurred the landscape, dulling the glow of streetlights in the distance. He shoved his hands into his pockets and paced to the kitchen to make a cup of tea.

While the kettle boiled, he tried calling Diana again.

It was no use, she wasn't answering — in fact, it went straight to voicemail as it'd been doing for two long hours. She might've forgotten to charge it or switched it off for some reason. Or she might be hurt, and unable to answer the phone.

As much as he was frustrated and angry by what she'd done all those years ago when she gave him up for adoption and didn't tell Andy he was a father, he couldn't help worrying about her. What if she'd lost her roof, been knocked down, slipped and fallen? Any number of things could've happened and perhaps no one knew because they were busy dealing with the cyclone.

The anger he'd felt was pushed aside by fear for her safety. He wouldn't be able to bear it if anything happened to her now after the way he'd left things between them the last time they spoke.

With a shake of his head, he grabbed his car keys and headed for the garage. He had to drive over there and check on her or he wouldn't be able to get to sleep that night.

The drive over to Diana's took much longer than usual. He had to detour several times around water across the road, and then around a fender-bender on the corner of Diana's street. Gusts of wind threatened to shift his car from the road several times, and he could hardly see the road ahead with the heavy rain that pushed the wipers to their limit.

Finally, he pulled up to Diana's house. It sat in darkness with no lights on. A streetlamp nearby issued a soft glow that illuminated one side of the house. He climbed from the car, pulling his raincoat on as he did. Zipping it up, Ben jogged up the footpath to Diana's front steps. He stopped before climbing them and peered up at the roof with a frown; something was off.

He took a few steps back, then gaped. A tree branch had fallen from a nearby tree and crushed one side of the roof — a few leaves poked over the gutter. In the dim light it was difficult to see the branch or how much damage it'd caused, but he didn't stop to look more closely.

It only took him a few strides to reach the front door. He turned the handle and found it locked. With a closed fist he pounded on the timber.

"Diana! Diana! Open up, it's Ben!"

There was no response. He cupped hands to the glass beside the door to look inside. It was too dark to be able to see much of anything, other than the table in the entryway with the delicately hand-painted vase filled with fresh flowers.

"Diana!"

He ran around the side of the house, through the gate and to the back door. It slid open with a little pressure and he sighed in relief.

"Diana! Where are you?"

A whimper in the living room drew him in that direction. He flicked a light switch, but there was no light. The power must've been knocked out.

He found her on the floor, with remnants of roof and plaster scattered around her. Rain drip-dropped around her. One leg was twisted at an impossible angle, and her eyes were shut.

Ben hunched over her, checking her vitals. The carpet beneath him was soaked with water. Diana's skin was cold, her lips blue.

"Diana, it's Ben — I'm here, don't worry you're going to be fine."

Her eyes blinked open. "Ben?"

He nodded, his throat tightening at the sight of her pale face and the disoriented look in her eyes.

"Yes, it's me. I'm going to take you to the hospital, okay?"

She gave a subtle nod of her head, letting her eyes drift shut again.

"Can you sit or stand?" He had to know how bad her injuries were; if her back was injured he didn't want to move her.

She shook her head. "My leg."

"Can you move your toes? Your fingers?"

She did both as he watched with relief. She'd already shaken her head and spoken to him, so it seemed like the leg was the main injury, possibly the only one.

When he lifted her, with both hands beneath her armpits, she cried out from the pain. They didn't get far before he gently lowered her back to the ground.

"I'm sorry," he said.

"It's okay," she puffed. "I'm just glad you're here. Thank you for coming. I know you're angry with me." The grimace on her face belied the pain she was in.

"Let's not talk about all that right now." He choked back a wave of emotion. "Not now. I've got to get you some help. Maybe we should call an ambulance," he suggested, wondering how he'd get her to the car on his own.

"No, they'll be run off their feet tonight. Rupert's wheelchair is in the garage."

It had been stashed in front of Diana's vehicle. He wheeled it into the living room and helped Diana into it with a lot of grunting and puffing on both their parts.

Finally, she was seated in the wheelchair, her face paler still, her teeth clamped down on her lower lip.

"You okay?" he asked, setting the footrests in place.

She pushed her lips into a half-smile. "Fighting fit."

"Let's go then."

* * *

AT THE HOSPITAL, Ben waited with Diana until a doctor was free to examine her. It'd been three hours since he found her when, finally, she was taken away to be X-rayed. He waited, elbow resting on his knees, hands in fists. He was exhausted. The emotion and stress of the past few hours had taken its toll on him and all he wanted to do was go to bed.

"Mr Silver?" A nurse strode towards him, her brown eyes full of kindness.

"Yes?" he stood to his feet.

"Your mother is doing fine. She fractured her tibia in two places. We're applying a cast right now and she'll be ready to go home shortly."

"Surgery?" he asked.

"No surgery needed. The doctor managed to align the bones beautifully. The break was a clean one and he thinks it should heal without any further intervention. She'll have to wear the cast for six weeks, then we'll take another X-ray to determine how it's healing and if she should continue with the cast or have it removed."

He sighed and rubbed his hands over his face, feeling the exhaustion creeping into his bones. "That's good news."

"You can see her when she's finished. She'll be out in a few minutes."

Diana was wheeled into the waiting room ten minutes later by an orderly. She offered him a tired smile. Her eyes were sunken and there were dark smudges beneath them.

He squatted in front of her, took a hand in between his. "Ready to go home?"

She nodded. "What about the roof?"

"You can stay with me until we get it fixed," he said, without thinking. It made sense, but the words surprised him as they came from his mouth.

"Thank you, Ben." Her voice broke on the words. "You're a wonderful son, I don't deserve…"

He swallowed the emotion that welled up his throat and glistened in his eyes. "We're family."

They drove home together, the quiet between them comfortable and warm. Finally, she spoke.

"How did you know — to come to my house, I mean?"

"I called you for about two hours straight — your home number wasn't working at all, and your mobile went to voicemail. At first I thought you might be avoiding my calls."

"I would never do that, honey." She reached out a hand to pat his arm. "No matter what."

He smiled in the dark. "That's good to know. Anyway, finally I couldn't take the suspense anymore. I had to find out what was going on."

"I'm glad you did."

"So am I. When I saw that branch on the roof- well, you gave me a fright."

"It gave me quite the fright too, I must say. I was reading in my armchair when there was an enormous crash on the roof and pieces of ceiling fell all around me. I got up to run and tripped over the side table. I thought the whole world was crashing in on me."

"I'll bet," he responded.

"If you hadn't thought to check on me, who knows how long I would've lay there. The roof might've caved in on me with all that rain coming in as well. Things could've gone much worse if it weren't for you." She squeezed his arm. "Thank you."

"I'm glad you're okay."

"I am too. I'm worried about the house — all that rain coming through the hole in the roof."

He sighed. "After I get you settled at my house, I'll go back and see if I can secure a tarp over the hole to keep the rain out until we're able to get a roofer to fix it."

She sighed. "Thank you, Ben. That would make me feel better, although I hope you'll be careful."

"I promise," he said.

He pulled into his garage and helped Diana into the house and got her settled in the guest bedroom. He made her hot chocolate and a toasted sandwich with ham and cheese and carried it to her bedroom, but found her fast asleep beneath the covers. It was late and he hadn't eaten anything since breakfast, so he sat in the kitchen and ate the meal he'd prepared for Diana.

After he'd washed the dishes, he tugged on his raincoat and found a tarpaulin in the garage, along with a ladder, a torch, and the tools he'd need to secure the tarp in place on the roof, and drove to Diana's house once again.

It took him an hour to manoeuvre the tarp into place over the hole. Finally, it was fixed in place with some staples from his staple gun and a few strategically placed bricks.

While he worked, he thought about Diana and the things they'd spoken of the last time he'd come to her house. He'd been angry, but was it warranted? Perhaps it was, he realised with a slump of his shoulders — but it wouldn't change anything. Neither one of them could go back in time or fix the past even if they'd like to.

She'd been so young, and he couldn't imagine what he might've done in her position at that age. He'd been looking at the situation from his perspective — as a man in his forties. Of course he'd have reacted differently; he was mature, self-sufficient, and able to make his own decisions. She hadn't been in that position. And perhaps he still might've reacted differently than she had, but there was still nothing that could be done about it. Dwelling on the past wouldn't help either one of them move on with their lives, nor would it build the relationships with Diana and Andy he wanted so much to have.

It was time for him to forgive. And as the decision passed through his mind, he realised he already had.

CHAPTER 29

CINDY

*W*ith her feet up on a chair positioned in front of the folding chair she was seated on, Cindy rolled up her jeans until the denim was above both knees. Both legs were red and grazed, mostly across her kneecaps. Her hands were tender to the touch as well.

With a grimace, she reached for the antiseptic ointment and a ball of cotton wool. She'd found a quiet room at the evacuation centre. It was a storage room, packed to the gills with boxes and stacks of chairs, but it would have to do for now. All she wanted was a little peace and quiet so she could doctor her wounds without being asked a million inconvenient questions about how she'd been hurt and why she hadn't seen a paramedic.

She didn't need to bother the paramedics with such nonsense. After all, she'd only grazed her hands and knees. It'd happened to her a dozen times in her life before and likely would again now she was getting older. If she was being truthful, it alarmed her how easily she'd lost her balance in helping Keisha to the side of the road. One of the many joys of growing older, she surmised.

Just as she wiped ointment across one knee and picked up a bandage to cover it, there was a knock at the door and Athol pushed it ajar and peeked through the gap.

"Cindy? They said you were in here. What on earth happened to you?"

She sighed, shook her head. "It's nothing. I fell, but I'm fine. What are you doing here?"

"I thought you'd like to know we found Rose's family. They're on their way to get her. So, I came looking for you. I haven't heard from you in hours and you're not answering your phone. I was worried. One of the kids said they thought they saw you come in here."

She smiled and applied the bandage with a quick flick of the wrist. "Well, that's very kind of you to think of me, but I'm fine. As you can clearly see. And thank you for the news about Rose."

He kissed her cheek, sat beside her on a box. "You're welcome. But you're not exactly fine."

"Only a few scrapes. Nothing serious."

He smiled, took her hands in his and reached for the ointment. "Let me finish up for you. Someone has to take care of you."

She sighed. "I'm fine, I promise."

"I know you are, but you're so busy looking after everyone else. Once in a while you need to be taken care of."

She had to admit it felt nice to have Athol caring for her, his gentle voice a balm to her agitated soul. Why was she so agitated? She wasn't sure exactly, but it probably had something to do with what'd happened to Keisha, how the woman had looked so vulnerable in the back of the ambulance. Ever since Andy begged Cindy to give him another chance, she'd wondered if he'd ended things with Keisha, but hadn't been game to call him and find out.

Turns out, they were still together — at least it certainly seemed that way. He was up to his old tricks — sweet talking one woman, while in a relationship with another. Only this time *she* was the other woman, and she didn't like how that felt. It'd been flattering to hear his words, to see his sincere and warm smile — the same smile that'd weakened her knees all those years ago when they were both teenagers falling in love.

But now she knew better.

He was a charmer — always had been, and it seemed he always would be. She felt bad for Keisha, who possibly had no idea what he'd been up to — the things he'd said to Cindy, or that he wanted to resume their marriage.

But that wasn't something she wanted or needed to revisit. She'd lost enough years to his lies. There was no way she'd return to that life — to always wondering where he was, who he was with, whether he'd be home. She may not have known for sure about his infidelities, but she hadn't trusted him completely the way she'd wanted to. There'd been too many small things that didn't make sense, stories that didn't ring true, receipts that didn't add up.

"Thank you," she said.

Athol bandaged her hands, then turned them over, and kissed the back of each, one at a time. Then, he bandaged her other knee and helped roll her jeans back into place.

"You're welcome, my darling."

His words warmed her heart. It was a different kind of love, this mature joining of two lives. It wasn't the over-heated infatuation of two teenagers who couldn't stand to be apart for more than a few minutes at a time, who couldn't keep their hands to themselves when they were together. It was a friendship that grew deeper whenever they were together, an enjoyment of each other's company. Respect and affection with roots so deep she almost couldn't pinpoint when it'd begun to shift from platonic to romantic.

And it was everything she'd wanted for so long. Everything she needed at this moment in time. No anxiety or looking for truth in the midst of lies. No mistrust or anger. A relationship based on only the good things — love, peace, and hope for a solid and secure future together.

She cupped his cheek with her bandaged hand. "You're a gem."

"So, tell me, how did you manage to fall — were you doing too much out there in the centre? Carrying something heavy perhaps? You know you shouldn't really be doing things like that, there are other people out there who can—"

"No, nothing like that," she interrupted him, standing to her feet and noticing the stiffness of bruising made it harder to walk after sitting still for a few minutes. "Ugh, that hurts."

"I think we should go home," he said. "It's three a.m., and I'm going to tuck you into bed, then sleep in the guest room if that's okay? I'd like to make you breakfast and check on you every now and then. You didn't hit your head, did you?"

He slid an arm around her waist as they walked — although she shuffled mostly — out of the storage room and towards the exit. The evacuation centre was bathed in darkness, with only a few nightlights on around the edges of the large, open space. Deep breathing and light snoring sounds drifted from sleeping bags and mats. A few children whispered and giggled.

"That sounds good to me," she said. "I'm utterly exhausted, and I don't think they need me here anymore."

"You still didn't answer my question." He stopped, pulled her around to face him, his eyes searching hers.

"I was at the cafe, making sure it was locked up and everyone went home. I saw Keisha crossing the street — she was bowled over by a flyaway umbrella. One of those big, heavy suckers. It knocked her out, I think. Anyway, she wasn't moving, and visibility was low. I went to help get her out of the road. We were almost mowed down by a delivery truck, and I fell helping her up onto the curb. Like I said, it wasn't a big deal. I shouldn't have fallen really; I suppose I'm older than I think I am." She grimaced. "Still, it was hard to balance what with the rushing water, rain in my face, and slippery tarmac."

Athol's eyes widened, and he shook his head slowly. "You risked your life to save hers."

She huffed. "I don't know about that."

"You did. She'd have been run over if it weren't for you. Both of you might've been run over. I don't — "

He hesitated. "You risked your life for the woman who ran off with your husband?"

Cindy's eyebrows arched. "Well, I suppose that's true, although I didn't really think of it like that at the time. I had to help her. That's the only thing that was going through my head."

His eyes glistened in the darkness. "You're remarkable, Cindy Flannigan."

She cocked her head. "I am?"

He laughed softly, taking her face between his hands and kissing the tip of her nose, then her lips. "Yes, you are. You could've died tonight or been seriously wounded by that truck — all because you wanted to save Keisha. A woman to whom you owed nothing, a woman who arguably destroyed the relationship you had with your husband. You're a good person, and I'm glad to have the chance to be part of your life."

He kissed her again, deeper this time, his passion igniting something within her that'd long lain dormant.

"I'm glad too," she replied.

He tucked his arm around her waist again, letting her lean on him as they walked. She hobbled slowly, feeling safe in his embrace, her heart swelling at the memory of his words and his kiss.

As they stepped outside, the steadily falling rain wet her face. Athol opened an umbrella above them, offered her a grin, then wound his arm around her again, holding the umbrella in place with his other hand. The irritation she'd felt — over her day, her life, her relationships, the cafe — wavered then drifted off on the humid night air leaving a satisfied smile on her face.

CHAPTER 30

REBECCA

*I*t was late but Rebecca couldn't sleep. She'd finally made it home and now it felt as though her stomach would implode and eat itself if she didn't get some food — and junky snacks wouldn't do. Chips, lamingtons, crackers, coffee — it was all she'd lived on for most of the day. She needed a meal, something healthy and substantial.

She poured a packet of pasta into boiling water then searched in the pantry for a jar of pesto. Freshly sliced chicken pieces waited on the cutting board on the bench, beside a plate of diced vegetables, onion, and garlic.

Her stomach clenched and growled so loud she was certain the neighbours would hear it. Next, the onion, garlic and olive oil went into a frying pan. The scent made her mouth water, before she added the rest of the vegetables and fried them lightly.

By the time the pasta was finished cooking the vegetables were perfectly sautéed. Rebecca tipped it all into a bowl, mixed it around with a generous dollop of basil pesto, and topped it with a sprinkle of parmesan before carrying the bowl to the dining table.

As she sat and spooned a serving of the steaming hot pasta into her bowl, a gigantic yawn threatened to split her face in two. She needed to get some sleep because she had to be back in the office first thing. The full force of the cyclone may have waned — according to news reports it'd diverted back out to sea — but it was still raining heavily, and there was likely to be flooding in parts of town, and nearby farming communities. No doubt there'd be plenty for her and the other police officers to do for days yet in the after-math of the storm.

She took a bite of pasta, the flavour of the fresh vegetables, garlic, and pesto bursting onto her tongue. Her eyes drifted shut and she savoured her meal, chewing slowly and enjoying a few moments of peace.

As she scraped up the last bite of pasta from her bowl, there was a knock at the door. Her brow furrowed. It was three thirty in the morning, who would be knocking at her door? Adrenaline burst into her veins, pushing the sleepiness aside.

A text message flashed across the screen of her phone. "Are you up? I'm at your door, want to talk."

It was Franklin. The nerves she'd felt, a reminder of living in a hyper alert state all those years with Jake hunting her down and taking out his frustration on her ribcage, faded as quickly as they'd come. Instead, they were replaced by butterflies in her stomach — they hadn't had a chance to really talk about what'd happened between them and where things might go next. Other than the brief conversation at the evacuation centre, of course. Which didn't really count since they'd had no privacy.

She smoothed her hair back with both hands, carried her bowl to the sink and then strode to the door.

When it opened, she saw Franklin at the end of the walkway behind the restaurant, about to go downstairs. He glanced up at her and smiled.

"I hope I didn't wake you."

A shake of the head and he walked towards her.

"Good. I finished up at the station and wanted to see you. When I got here I suddenly realised how late it was — or early, whichever way you look at it."

"I wasn't sleeping, I was eating dinner," she replied.

He quirked an eyebrow. "Something smells delicious."

"You hungry? I've got plenty."

"Are you sure? I can come back at a more decent hour."

"It's fine, come in. You can eat, we can talk, then I have to get some sleep because my boss expects me at work in a few hours."

"He sounds like a real drag."

"Oh, you have no idea." She shut the door behind them.

* * *

FRANKLIN ATE a bowl of pasta and they chatted about the day — what happened, good and bad, what went wrong, the dramas of dealing with a community in turmoil. It felt good to be able to offload some of the things churning around in her mind. His sensible, patient advice calmed her spirits as always.

"That was delicious. Thanks, Proby." He stood and stretched his arms over his head in a yawn. "But I should get home, see if I can catch a few hours of sleep before I head back into the station."

"Me too."

She followed him to the front door. He opened it and faced her with the hint of a smile playing around his lips, his brown eyes sleepy and half-lidded.

He reached for her hands, threaded his fingers through hers. "I like spending time with you."

She nodded, grinning.

"And I want to do more of it," he continued.

"Oh yeah?"

"Definitely." He leaned down to kiss her lips.

He smelled of pasta and pesto, and his kiss awakened a passion within her she fought to restrain.

His eyes were smoky with desire when he stepped back, still watching her. "I don't think we can go back to being just friends after a kiss like that."

She laughed. "Highly unlikely that would work out for us."

"Impossible really."

"So, I guess we'll have to see where this thing between us goes, then."

He shook his head. "No, I don't think so."

Her eyes narrowed. "Oh, I thought we were on the same page."

"Not really, because I *know* where I want things between us to go."

Her heart skipped a beat, she swallowed hard.

"I've fought against the attraction between us, of course. Did everything I could to push you away, or to keep a wall between us. And I'm sorry for that." He kissed her again.

She didn't know why, but her throat tightened with tears. He'd never opened up to her this way before, never showed her how vulnerable he could be.

"Thank you for telling me that, I know it must've been hard."

"That's the thing — it wasn't hard. Something's changed between us, something really important now you're no longer hiding your past from me. For a long time, I knew you were hiding something, but I wasn't sure what it was — so I didn't think I could trust you. Now, I know I can. I trust you completely."

She reached up to pull him down to her for another kiss. This time her lips searched his, full of the passion she'd pent up for so long.

"I know it's quick, and it's probably going to be a complete surprise to you so you don't have to say anything, but I love you Bec," he said.

Her eyes widened and she leaned against his chest, feeling the steady heartbeat on her cheek.

"I love you too, Franklin."

He pulled back until they were looking into each other's eyes. One hand cupped her chin, tipping her face towards his. His eyes sparkled in the dull light.

"I want to spend our lives together, to be a family. Will you marry me?"

Her heart thundered against her ribcage. Her head was swimming from the recent kiss, her mind unable to land on any thought long enough to understand it other than one — she loved him, wanted to be with him always and couldn't imagine her life without him.

"Yes," she whispered.

And he kissed her again.

CHAPTER 31

MEG

The baby's plump cheeks were tinged with a rosy hue. Meg cradled Amari in her arms, unable to wipe the smile from her face. It was a month since her birth and they'd finally been allowed to bring her home with them the previous day. She'd spent the full four weeks in the special care nursery, and they'd visited her every day wishing and hoping they could bring her home.

Now she was here, Meg felt as though she was living in some kind of dream. It didn't seem real. The stresses of pumping, visiting the hospital, leaving for the day, and missing Amari were finished. They were a family, living together in their cosy little unit beside the beach, and she couldn't be happier. Brad was more chipper than ever. She'd never seen him so delighted about anyone or anything. Amari truly already had him wrapped around her tiny, pudgy finger.

"I'm going to uni," he said, wheeling into the bedroom.

He spotted Amari in her arms and wheeled closer to reach for the baby's hand. Her fingers immediately curled shut around one of his.

"Okay, well, have a good day," replied Meg.

He groaned. "I'm going to miss the two of you."

"I know, but I suppose you've got to get back to your normal life at some point. Otherwise, we'll all have to live under a bridge and starve to death."

"Well, when you put it like that... But what if she does something while I'm not here? She might smile or reach for something. She's going to do things for the first time, and I'll miss it," he said.

"I promise to make videos for you and take about a zillion photos a day. Does that help?"

He sighed. "I suppose it'll have to do."

"Besides, you'll be home this evening, and on weekends."

"True. All right, I'll see you later."

He kissed them both goodbye and left. When he shut the door behind him, the unit fell into complete silence. In her arms, Amari's eyes drifted shut. Meg rocked her back and forth, humming a lullaby as she watched her baby girl's adorable round face.

Her little eyelashes formed dark half-moons against her pale cheeks, her button nose was temptingly kissable, and her lips pulled suddenly into a half-smile as though she was grinning in her sleep.

Meg leaned forward to kiss her forehead. "Amari Taylor, you are absolutely perfect."

The unit door slammed shut.

Meg frowned, walked slowly from the bedroom into the kitchen. "What on earth?"

"I couldn't leave," explained Brad, as he set his

backpack filled with textbooks and a laptop on the ground by the front door.

She shook her head. "But—"

"I'll go tomorrow, I promise. But today, I want to take Amari to the beach together. We'll have a family picnic."

"I think she's a bit small for the beach, honey."

"We can stay in the shade, and I'll just point it out to her."

She didn't want to argue with him when he was clearly so excited. It meant a lot to Brad to share his beloved ocean with his daughter, so she agreed. Together they packed a picnic basket with food and a blanket. Then, with Brad in his beach wheelchair and Amari in her pram, they set off together towards the Emerald Cove beach.

As Meg pushed the pram along the footpath, her heart soared with joy. A few months ago, she would never have imagined how good it could feel to have her little family with her, on their way to their very first beach picnic. Even with all of the challenges they'd faced over the past year, she couldn't be happier than she was in that moment.

They'd dealt with so much after Brad's accident. When they'd feared for Amari's health after their scan, Meg hadn't been sure she could cope with a sick or disabled child in addition to everything else life had thrown her way. But Amari was a healthy and happy little baby, despite her premature birth. It was amazing how well she'd recovered, and Meg marvelled every day over the way she grew and changed.

Brad looked up at her, his muscled arms bulging in his sleeves as he rolled the wheelchair forward. "Can you believe how happy we are?"

She chuckled. "I was thinking the exact same thing."

"I wasn't sure we'd make it. There were times..." he began, shaking his head.

"I know what you mean. But we got through those hard days."

He nodded with lips pursed. She stopped beside him and rested a hand on his shoulder.

He pulled her down to him and kissed her lips. "Thank you."

She smiled. "For what?"

"Being you."

"Well, I don't have much choice in the matter. But you're welcome."

"I don't know what I'd have done without you."

Joy trickled into her heart. "Right back atcha, honey."

She kissed his lips, lingering a moment longer to savour the feel of him. Her heart thudded and her head felt light.

Then they continued on their way, the baby sleeping soundly in the pram.

CINDY

"I'm glad you invited me to lunch," said Andy, taking a bite of the bread roll on his side plate.

Cindy nodded, buttered her roll, and glanced at her ex-husband, working up the nerve to say the things that needed saying.

She could've ignored it, the tension that'd developed between them since their last conversation at her house, but it was time to address it, to resolve things between them once and for all.

"I'm glad you came. It's so nice to see you." She meant it. He was always fun to spend time with, that hadn't changed. And regardless of the way things had turned out, or the wrongs he'd done to her during their marriage and since, he'd always have a special place in her heart. After all, he was her first love, the father of all three of her children, and the man she'd spent most of her life with.

But now it was time for them both to put the past to rest and move forward with their lives.

The cafe was full of diners, the sun was shining, and the destruction of the cyclone had been cleaned up over the past few weeks. The town gleamed like new, apart from the tree in the median strip beside the cafe that was missing half its trunk and a large branch.

Cindy glanced through the climbing vines that lined the outdoor seating area across the street at the brand-new portico entry to Foodstore. Marg would soon recover from her injuries but for now she was still hobbling around behind the deli counter with a boot on one foot, the cast reaching up beyond her knee to protect the healing fractures in her leg.

She linked her fingers together in front of her salad plate.

"I wanted to talk to you, and I know how much you enjoy lunch at the cafe."

He grinned, his dimples flashing. "I do love the lunch menu."

"I wanted to address our last conversation."

He nodded slowly, chewing on a bite of chicken. "Yes, I've been thinking about that little talk as well."

"The thing is, you know I'll always care for you."

He stopped chewing; his eyes narrowed. "I'm not sure I like where this is going, my love."

"But I'm not anymore — your love, that is. I'm not your love, I'm your ex-wife."

"But—"

She raised a hand to quiet him. "That was your choice and you made it. Now, I don't hold it against you. At least, I don't anymore. But I can't go backwards. My life has changed a lot since you walked out on me, and I don't want to go back to the way things were. I've grown, I've changed, I've paid off a lot of debt."

He rolled his eyes. "Is that what this is about?"

"No, it's not about that. I'm trying to explain to you how I feel. I've moved on. I suppose that's the crux of it. I've moved on and my life has changed, I've changed. You'll always be part of my family and I care about you, but I don't want to be married to you anymore. I'm sorry, Andy. I know that's not what you wanted to hear."

His nostrils flared. "But we've got history."

"Yes, we do. Nothing will change that or take away from it."

"You don't care?"

She shook her head. "Of course I do. I care about you, about the kids, about the life we built together. But I don't want to go back to that life anymore. The kids are grown, you've moved on, and it's time for me to move on as well."

"I can't say I'm happy about that, but I suppose I understand." He leaned back in his chair, arms folded over his chest.

"You'll see, it's the right decision to make. We wouldn't be happy together. Not anymore. I put up with a lot of things to make our marriage work, over the years. Didn't speak up when I should've, kept my complaints to myself, didn't criticise you when I felt you deserved it. I wouldn't be able to hold back those words anymore. Not with everything that's happened and after enjoying my own company for over a year."

He chuckled. "Well, I suppose that makes sense."

"No hard feelings?" she offered him a hand.

He shook it. "No hard feelings."

"I'm glad you're back in the Cove, Andy. I know the kids love spending time with you. And I hear you've been able to get to know Ben a little bit."

He nodded. "I have to admit, I'm loving being back home and seeing all of the kids more frequently. And Ben is, well, he's a wonderful man. Still hard to believe he's my son, but I'm grateful I've had the chance to get to know him, even if I did miss out on so many years of his life."

"Have you spoken to Diana lately?"

He nodded, sighed. "I had coffee with her last week. I told her I forgave her, which let me tell you — was a hard thing to do after what she robbed Ben and me of. But I do forgive her. I know she was young, and I'm not sure I would've done anything differently at the time, anyway. We made up, she kissed my cheek, and all is well with the world, so you don't have to worry about that anymore, my dear."

She smiled, her throat aching just a little. "I'm glad to hear it. We're too old, and have known each other too long to let grudges form between any of us."

"You're right about that," he said with a wink.

He took the last bite of his salad, stood, and placed his napkin on the table. "I'm going to head out, if you don't mind. I need some time to process what you've said."

She stood as well, squeezed his arm. "Of course. I'll see you around town."

He nodded. "Goodbye, Cindy."

She watched him go, her vision blurred by tears. It was hard to let go of the past and what they'd shared together, even if she knew it was the right thing for her.

He'd moved out of their home so long ago it felt normal not to have him around. But still, this was the first time it'd seemed final. Her words had shut a door that'd been ajar ever since he left without an explanation — always the possibility that he'd come back and they'd patch things up between them to start again.

"You finished?" asked Athol, striding to her and looping his arms around her waist.

She nodded.

"Are you okay?" he asked, kissing the tip of her nose.

"It's finally over — finally *feels* over."

"And that's a good thing?"

"That's a good thing," she affirmed with a smile. "It's a little sad, but it's definitely good."

He offered her his hand. She took it and together they strolled from the cafe.

"Let's take a walk," he suggested.

As they wandered down the main street of Emerald Cove, Athol's fingers linked with hers, Cindy felt a new excitement for the days ahead. Her life was no longer a story already written; she had a chance to do something new and she wasn't going to waste that opportunity. She didn't know what the future held, but she anticipated the unexpected in a way she'd never been able to do before — with the understanding that anything was possible.

"I listed my house this week," she said.

Athol glanced her way, one eyebrow quirked. "Did you? Well, that's exciting."

"And I put an offer on that chalet-style house over on Cliffside Drive. They accepted the offer. So, I'm moving."

He laughed. "That calls for a celebration."

She nodded. "Yes it does. Time for new beginnings."

"And new adventures," he added.

"Yes indeed."

REBECCA

The chapel of the church was bathed in sunlight. It danced, dappled and golden, over the wooden pews, glancing off the white roses that sat in bunches beside the first row.

Rebecca slipped her hands into Franklin's, her face beaming. Franklin kissed her mother's cheek which was wet with tears.

"Thank you, Liz," he whispered.

She nodded, her grey hair bobbing. "Bless you both."

Mum turned and sat in the first row besides Beth, whose red-rimmed eyes were fixed firmly on Rebecca's. She smiled at her sister, then faced Franklin, her stomach in knots.

She'd never been one to act impulsively. But here

they were, a month after he'd proposed, getting married in front of family and friends.

The minister began reciting the vows, but Rebecca couldn't focus on what he was saying. Instead, her attention was fixed on Franklin's face — his kind eyes, strong jaw, and the hint of mischief in his smile that was not only addictive but contagious.

The past month had been a whirlwind for her. They'd spent every moment together they could, and the more she got to know him — the man rather than the boss — the more she loved him. The emotional walls he'd used to keep her at arm's length were gone and instead he'd become warm, loving, and always kind. She couldn't imagine a man better suited to her than he was.

After the service, they walked hand in hand down the aisle. Her heart swelled at the sight of family and friends cheering them on and grinning from ear to ear.

"I'm so glad we stayed in the Cove to get married," she said. "I considered Sydney, but it wouldn't have been the same."

He squeezed her hand. "Thank you for agreeing to do it in Dad's church — for some reason, it makes me feel as though he's here with us in some small way."

She faced him, looped her hands around his neck and stared into his eyes. "Anything for you, my love."

"Really?" he asked, his eyes twinkling. "I may test you out on that later."

Her cheeks flushed pink. "You're impossible."

He laughed. "I think it's best you know this about me from the beginning. Better to be completely honest and upfront in relationships. At least, that's my motto."

He kissed her, and she let her eyes drift shut to drink in the moment. Friends and family clapped them on the back and offered congratulations. Each of them turned to hug friends, kiss cheeks, and thank people for attending. All the while, one of her hands remained entwined in Franklin's. Grounded to her husband, to the new life she'd dived into without a moment's hesitation. It wasn't like her, but for some reason she'd known it was exactly what she needed. And she was no longer afraid of what might come — since she now knew she had everything she needed, within herself and with Franklin by her side, to tackle whatever lay ahead.

THE END

ALSO BY LILLY MIRREN

THE WARATAH INN SERIES

The Waratah Inn

Wrested back to Cabarita Beach by her grandmother's sudden death, Kate Summer discovers a mystery buried in the past that changes everything.

One Summer in Italy

Reeda leaves the Waratah Inn and returns to Sydney, her husband, and her thriving interior design business, only to find her marriage in tatters. She's lost sight of what she wants in life and can't recognise the person she's become.

The Summer Sisters

Set against the golden sands and crystal clear waters of Cabarita Beach three sisters inherit an inn and discover a mystery about their grandmother's past that changes everything they thought they knew about their family...

Christmas at The Waratah Inn

Liz Cranwell is divorced and alone at Christmas. When her friends convince her to holiday at The Waratah Inn, she's dreading her first Christmas on her own. Instead she discovers that strangers can be the balm to heal the wounds of a lonely heart in this heartwarming Christmas story.

EMERALD COVE SERIES

Cottage on Oceanview Lane

When a renowned book editor returns to her roots, she rediscovers her strength & her passion in this heartwarming novel.

Seaside Manor Bed & Breakfast

The Seaside Manor Bed and Breakfast has been an institution in Emerald Cove for as long as anyone can remember. But things are changing and Diana is nervous about what the future might hold for her and her husband, not to mention the historic business.

Bungalow on Pelican Way

Moving to the Cove gave Rebecca De Vries a place to hide from her abusive ex. Now that he's in jail, she can get back to living her life as a police officer in her adopted hometown working alongside her intractable but very attractive boss, Franklin.

Chalet on Cliffside Drive

At forty-four years of age, Ben Silver thought he'd never find love. When he moves to Emerald Cove, he does it to support his birth mother, Diana, after her husband's sudden death. But then he meets Vicky.

Christmas in Emerald Cove

The Flannigan family has been through a lot together. They've grown and changed over the years and now have a blended and extended family that doesn't always see eye to eye. But this Christmas they'll learn that love can overcome all of the pain and differences of the past in this inspiring Christmas tale.

HOME SWEET HOME SERIES

Home Sweet Home

Trina is starting over after a painful separation from her husband of almost twenty years. Grief and loss force her to return to her hometown where she has to deal with all of the things she left behind to rebuild her life, piece by piece; a hometown she hasn't visited since high school graduation.

No Place Like Home

Lisa never thought she'd leave her high-profile finance job in the city to work in a small-town bakery. She also never expected to still be single in her forties.

GLOSSARY OF TERMS

Dear reader,

Since this book is set in Australia there may be some terms you're not familiar with. I've included them below to help you out! I hope they didn't trip you up too much.

Cheers, Lilly xo

Terms

Barrister - lawyer who argues in court

Bonnet - car hood

Boot - car trunk

Brass - the people in charge

Chook - chicken

Fibro - cheap fibrous cement sheeting used for building houses

Firies - fire fighter

Footpath - sidewalk

"Love" - a term of endearment for friends and lovers alike

Tea - used to describe either a hot beverage made from leaves, or the evening meal

Unit - apartment or condo

Mobile - cell phone

Old codger - elderly person (term of endearment)

Proby - Probationary Constable

Rumpus room - den

Sarge - Sergeant

Stoked - Excited

Unit - apartment

Yum cha - dim sum served from pushable carts

ABOUT THE AUTHOR

Lilly Mirren is a USA Today Bestselling author. She lives in Brisbane, Australia with her husband and three children.

She always dreamed of being a writer and is now living that dream. When she's not writing, she's chasing her children or spending time with friends.

Her books combine heartwarming storylines with achingly realistic characters readers can't get enough of. Her debut series, The Waratah Inn, set in the delightful Cabarita Beach, hit the USA Today Bestseller list and since then, has touched the hearts of hundreds of thousands of readers across the globe.

Follow Lilly:

Website: www.lillymirren.com
Facebook: https://www.
facebook.com/authorlillymirren/
Twitter: https://twitter.com/lilly_mirren
BookBub: https://www.bookbub.com/authors/lilly-mirren

Instagram: https://www.instagram.com/lilly_mirren/
Binge Books: https://bingebooks.com/author/lilly-
mirren